"Are you done with me being your practice boyfriend?" Dev asked.

The ball was in her court. Caitlyn understood that. But she couldn't help fear what would happen if she took the next step. They flirted, laughed, shared deeply personal thoughts. She didn't want to lose that. What if they slept together and it didn't work out?

"Yes. I don't want us to practice anymore." The words tumbled out of her before she could stop them.

He closed the distance between them and pressed his lips firmly to hers. His tongue flicked across her bottom lip and she lost all rational thought. Her entire body quivered, her core hot and desperate for his touch. This time she didn't hold back. She let her tongue tangle with his.

When the kiss wasn't enough, she twisted her body further and tucked a knee underneath her so she could get even closer...

* * *

Boyfriend Lessons by Sophia Singh Sasson is part of the Texas Cattleman's Club: Ranchers and Rivals series.

Dear Reader,

Thank you for taking the time to read my book. It is such an honor for me to write one of the Texas Cattleman's Club stories; even more so because I get to share a small piece of my culture with you. Dev and Caitlyn captured my heart and I hope they will make room in yours, too.

While Dev was born in the US, he struggles with some of the same things that I do as a first-generation immigrant. How do you integrate the Indian side of you with the American side? Why do you even feel like there are two sides of you? Reconciling his feelings for Caitlyn with his family expectations is a struggle I'm well familiar with. Caitlyn is someone for whom the emotional connection is even more important than the physical one, but it's hard to make that connection when you're not ready to open yourself up. I'm excited to share Dev and Caitlyn's journey with you.

Hearing from readers makes my day, so please email me at Sophia@SophiaSasson.com, tag me on Twitter (@sophiasasson), Instagram (@sophia_singh_sasson) or Facebook (/authorsophiasasson), or find me on Goodreads, BookBub (@sophiasinghsasson) or my website, www.sophiasasson.com.

Love,

Sophia

SOPHIA SINGH SASSON

BOYFRIEND LESSONS

Thank you to the awesome Harlequin Desire editorial team, in
particular Stacy Boyd and Charles Griemsman, who have always
given me a chance, and my agent, Barbara Rosenberg,
for always looking out for me.

It's lonely being an author, but the amazing community of
South Asian romance writers always keeps me going.

Last and most important, I wouldn't be an author without
the love and support of my husband. Love you, Tom!

HARLEQUIN®
DESIRE™

ISBN-13: 978-1-335-73564-5

Boyfriend Lessons

Copyright © 2022 by Harlequin Enterprises ULC

Special thanks and acknowledgment are given to Sophia Singh Sasson
for her contribution to the Texas Cattleman's Club: Ranchers and Rivals
miniseries.

Harlequin Enterprises ULC
22 Adelaide St. West, 41st Floor
Toronto, Ontario M5H 4E3, Canada
www.Harlequin.com

Printed in U.S.A.

Sophia Singh Sasson puts her childhood habit of daydreaming to good use by writing stories she wishes will give you hope, make you laugh, cry and possibly snort tea from your nose. She was born in Bombay, India, has lived in Canada and currently resides in Washington, DC. She loves to read, travel, bake, scuba dive, make candles and hear from readers. Visit her at www.sophiasasson.com.

Books by Sophia Singh Sasson

Harlequin Desire

Texas Cattleman's Club: Ranchers and Rivals

Boyfriend Lessons

Nights at the Mahal

Marriage by Arrangement
Running Away with the Bride

Harlequin Heartwarming

State of the Union

The Senator's Daughter
Mending the Doctor's Heart

Welcome to Bellhaven

First Comes Marriage

Visit her Author Profile page at Harlequin.com, or sophiasasson.com, for more titles.

You can also find Sophia on Facebook, along with other Harlequin Desire authors, at Facebook.com/harlequindesireauthors!

This book is dedicated to all those who've ever wondered—what's wrong with me?
The answer is absolutely nothing.
You are perfect as you are, and I hope you find that special someone who thinks so, too.

One

"So you just left?" Caitlyn Lattimore said incredulously. She was used to Alice's crazy dating experiences, but this one made her sit up in the pool lounger.

Alice slid her oversize sunglasses on top of her wavy blond hair, refilled her chardonnay glass and topped off Caitlyn, who had barely touched her first glass.

"The man ordered two appetizers, lobster for dinner and a bottle of wine from the reserve list. Then he pulls 'the left my wallet at home' crap. No, thank you. I told him I was going to the bathroom and then asked the waitress if I could escape through the kitchen door because he was a creep."

Her dating stories get scarier by the day.

Alice grabbed the bottle of suntan lotion and rubbed her arms. "I need to find a better dating site."

Caitlyn reached for the sunblock. It was early June, and the sun was strong. One touch of UV and her skin would turn shades browner. She had a number of Lattimore events to attend in the next month, and her makeup artist had just spent days perfecting the right shade of foundation for her. Alice called them rich girl problems, and Caitlyn agreed. She'd won the lottery when the Lattimores adopted her twenty-four years ago. Even now, they were sitting by the sparkling blue pool of the Lattimore ranch, their wine bottle perfectly chilled and a staff member readily available should they need anything else. Alice called it the Ritz Lattimore, but it was home for Caitlyn, one she loved not because of the luxuries, but because her family lived here.

"I wish I had your chutzpah. If that had happened to me, I'd have paid the bill and spent the night seething." Caitlyn said.

"Darlin', for that to happen to you, you'd need to actually go out on a date. To leave this gilded cage and venture into the smog and filth we mortals call the real world."

"You sound just like Alexa."

Alexa had left Royal for New York City, and then Miami, when she went to college and never looked back. She'd been home recently, though, for Victor Grandin's funeral.

Alice raised a brow. "I was sorry to hear about

Layla's grandfather dying. Victor Grandin was such a pillar in this community."

"He was. Alexa came home for the funeral and I suspect Layla would like Alexa to stay permanently, because her cutthroat lawyering skills will help our two families."

"Is this about that letter that came at the funeral? You never told me the full story."

Caitlyn's stomach roiled. "Turns out Heath Thurston is making a claim against the oil rights to the land beneath the Grandin and Lattimore ranches." It wasn't the claim that worried Caitlyn but the effect it was having on her family.

Alice leaned forward. "See, this is what happens when we don't see each other for a month—I miss all the juicy gossip."

"It's more than gossip. Those oil rights include the land that the Lattimore mansion is built on. Heath claims Daniel Grandin fathered Heath's late half-sister, Ashley, and that Daniel's dad gave Heath's mother Cynthia the oil rights. He says he found some of his mother's papers supporting the claim."

Alice's mouth hung open. Even she was speechless after that. The thought of what losing their family home would do to her siblings had consumed Caitlyn every second for the last month, since Victor Grandin's funeral.

"How did Ashley die?"

"In a car crash that also included her mother, Cynthia."

"Why did Victor Grandin Sr. give Cynthia the oil rights and not Ashley?"

"We don't know. And my grandfather signed the document, too, so he knew about it. Now he doesn't remember a thing, so Victor Grandin Jr. hired a private investigator for the two families to look into why they might have signed over the oil rights for our lands, and whether Daniel really fathered Cynthia's child."

Alice sat back, speechless once again. "Have you ever met Heath or his twin brother, Nolan?"

Caitlyn shook her head.

"I went to high school with them. They are hot. I'm talking freshly seared steak hot. I'd forgotten about Nolan, he left Royal but if he's back, that changes the dating scene." She wiggled her eyebrows at Caitlyn. "They're both single."

Caitlyn smiled. "There's enough drama in my family without me trying to date the men trying to destroy our ranch."

Caitlyn chewed on her lip. Alice was right about one thing—she needed to get a life; she was tired of her image as the quiet, shy woman who startled when a man sneezed next to her. Even though the last part was right. "Maybe I should sign up for one of these dating sites. Not all of yours have been that bad. What happened to the guy who sent you flowers and took you to meet his family?"

"He was fine, a bit boring in the sex department but I was willing to deal with that until he took a call with his mother while he was on top of me."

Caitlyn had just taken a sip of her wine, and it went flying out of her mouth, spraying all over the pool lounger. She covered her mouth in embarrassment.

Alice smiled and handed her one of the rolled hand towels from a basket on the table. Caitlyn wiped her mouth and the pool lounger. "You know not to do that to me when I'm drinking," Caitlyn said, laughing.

"Sorry, I forgot about that endearing habit of yours."

"The guy actually talked to his mom while you were in the middle of having sex?"

Alice nodded. "What's worse is he talked to her for a good two minutes, and wanted to continue on like it didn't make a difference."

"How could you not tell me about this?"

"That happened on the day of the Grandin funeral. I was so embarrassed I couldn't even think about it." Alice shook her head. "You and I need to meet men in real life. It's hard to suss out the creep factor online. It's singles' night at the Lone Star nightclub. How about we get all dressed up and go?"

I'd rather face down a pack of hungry wolves.

"You know that's not my scene. There aren't enough cocktails in the world to get me comfortable enough to talk to a strange man. It seems safer to start out with online chatting."

Alice shook her head. "Dating sites are not for you, darlin'. You need someone who's vetted, get some practice in before you go out into the world of vultures and mamas' boys."

Caitlyn nearly spit out her drink again. "I'll skip the mama's boy, but I could use someone who has the backbone to withstand the Lattimore siblings. The last time I went out on a date, Jonathan asked if he could have the guy's Social Security number to run a background check. The time before that, Jayden followed me to the restaurant where I was meeting a blind date. He didn't like the look of the guy, so he stayed parked on the street the entire time I was at dinner and followed us home."

Alice put her hand to her heart. "Your brothers are super sweet."

"No, they're overprotective. They don't pull that stuff with Alexa."

"Because she moved away." Alice took a sip of her wine. "I do have a nice, decent guy with whom you can practice your flirting skills." Alice smiled cheekily, and Caitlyn narrowed her eyes.

"There has to be something wrong with him or you would've dated him."

Alice laughed. "That would be really weird. I'm talking about Russ."

Caitlyn raised a brow. "Your brother, Russ? I thought you said he wasn't into serious dating."

Alice shifted on the lounger. "He's not, which is why he'd be the perfect person to practice your conversational skills. You two really haven't hung out, so he's like a strange man."

Caitlyn bit her lip. She didn't want to offend Alice,

but she'd never felt a spark with her brother, Russ. He was a nice enough guy, but he was just so *white*. Not that she had a problem dating white men. Her biological mother was white, but in the last couple of years she'd struggled with her identity, along with most of the country. Despite her closeness with Alice, her best friend didn't understand Caitlyn's struggle with being a woman of color. Alice had never been asked where she was from, as if her brown skin automatically meant that she was exotic or foreign. Caitlyn had struggled with that over the last two years, debating her own identity. Was she Black, white, both or neither? Whenever a form asked what her race or ethnicity was, she left it blank, because none of the categories fit her. That was the one thing she and Jax had in common. Her ex-boyfriend was also biracial, and he'd understood some of the things she'd struggled with. Yet it hadn't worked out with him, either. Maybe she really was a lost cause.

"Caitlyn, what's the harm? It's just Russ, and you could use the practice."

"I don't know…. Have you asked Russ?"

Alice shook her head reluctantly. "Look, he's coming home after months of travel. I was going to have dinner with him on Friday. Why don't you come? It'll just be the three of us. Low-key. No pressure. I'll be there to back you up and fill in if you stammer over your words or spit out your wine."

Caitlyn threw her dirty hand towel playfully at Alice. *What do I have to lose?* She was bored by the endless conversations about the fate of the Grandin and Lattimore ranches in her house and of making excuses about why she didn't date more. Ever since Layla Grandin and Josh Banks had gotten together, her family had been even more determined to see Caitlyn out and dating. She was tired of being pitied by her siblings. It was time to get over what had happened with Jax. It had been a year since they'd broken up. She'd been on a few dates since then—all failures, thanks to the scars Jax had left. She knew intellectually that Jax was just a bad dating experience, but it clung to her, haunted her thoughts at the most inappropriate times. It was time to replace those memories, even if it was with something meaningless.

"Come on, Caitlyn, what's the worst that can happen?"

She sighed. *That I'll hate Russ but you'll fall in love with the idea of me and Russ and it'll affect our friendship.*

"I'll order Italian from your favorite place," Alice said coaxingly.

"I'll come to dinner. As a friend. I'm not dating Russ."

Alice beamed. "Who said anything about dating? Think of it as a practice session."

"You've got to be kidding me." Alice glared at her phone.

"Trouble?" Caitlyn asked as she arranged the cutlery on Alice's table. Alice lived in a charming row house in the center of Royal. She had decorated it in a comfortable cottage style with soft pastel colors and wood furniture. Caitlyn had come early to help Alice with dinner preparations. She enjoyed the easy way she could make a salad in Alice's kitchen. At her house, the staff took it as an affront if she prepared her own food, feeling that they weren't meeting her standards.

"Russ is late, and he's bringing a friend to dinner."

Caitlyn smiled. While Russ was supposed to be her practice date tonight, it would serve Alice right if he brought another woman home with him. Caitlyn had suspected, but she now knew, that Alice hadn't told Russ she was setting them up.

"I'll set another place at the table," Caitlyn volunteered, her voice sugary sweet. "Don't worry, you have enough food to feed the entire block." If Russ was bringing a woman, Caitlyn could sit back and watch the two of them interact and take notes. The churning in her stomach slowed, and she opened a bottle of wine and poured two glasses. She didn't like to drink when she was anxious, but the evening was looking up.

"How dare Russ bring a woman." Alice seethed.

"Did you tell him he was here to give me boyfriend lessons?" Even as she said the words, Caitlyn realized how ridiculous the idea had been all along. There was no such thing as practicing dating skills. Was there?

She took a large sip from her glass, picturing herself taking notes as she watched Russ and his date converse during dinner as if she were sitting in a classroom. The idea made her giggle.

A half hour later, when the doorbell rang, both Alice and Caitlyn had polished off equal parts of an entire bottle of Bordeaux, and Caitlyn was looking forward to the evening.

Alice opened the door and greeted her brother. Caitlyn waited patiently on the gray leather couch, not wanting to interrupt the inevitable whispered shouting of Alice berating Russ for spoiling the date setup that he didn't know he was participating in. She felt bad for Russ and even worse for his poor date, who would have no idea what she had done to incur Alice's passive-aggressive wrath.

"I can't believe it's you!" Alice's squeals made Caitlyn sit up.

Before she could react, they all walked in, and Caitlyn nearly choked on her drink as she caught sight of the most beautiful man that she'd ever seen.

Two

Dev Mallik knew the moment he walked into Alice's apartment that Russ was going to hate him by the end of the night. He and Russ had been quite the pair in college, Dev with his dark hair, brooding green eyes and generally standoffish nature and Russ with his baby blues, dirty blond hair and the kind of aw-shucks face that made women stalk him after their relationship ended. Russ always got the girl and Dev was stuck entertaining the friend.

But their arrangement suited him just fine. He had enough drama with his family—he didn't need relationship issues to compound them. He preferred women who were vivacious, confident and ready to forget him after one night. Which was why Russ had convinced him to come to dinner at his sister's.

Apparently, Alice was prone to setting Russ up, and the last time he'd dated one of Alice's Royal friends, he'd ended up not being able to come home for six months in order to avoid running into the woman at the doorstep to his condo building. So, he'd brought Dev along tonight to distract the friend from Russ's irresistible charms.

Except, one look at Alice's friend as she put a hand to her delicate mouth and Dev's knees buckled. Before him was the most stunning woman he'd ever seen. She met his gaze and her deep brown eyes, brimming with innocence and laughter widened.

She stood slowly, and he noticed the wineglass in her hand tip forward, so he stepped toward her and placed his hand on her elbow to steady her arm.

Impossibly, her eyes widened some more, and he found himself mesmerized. Her lips parted and though he knew he was being rude, he couldn't help staring at how perfectly pink they were against her tanned skin. What would it be like to run his fingertips across their lusciousness?

Someone cleared their throat—Dev couldn't be sure whether it was Alice or Russ—but it seemed to jar the beautiful woman. She stepped away from him.

"Dev, this is my friend Caitlyn."

Caitlyn. He rolled the name on his tongue. The beautiful name suited her.

He smiled. "Nice to meet you." He extended his hand. She set the wineglass on a side table and took his hand. Her skin was silky soft and warm. It was the kind of hand he wanted to feel on his naked skin, and he held on to it a little too long.

Alice said something he didn't hear, and Caitlyn took her hand back.

"Russ, you remember Caitlyn," Alice introduced them.

Russ stepped forward. "Hey, Caitie, nice to see you again." Caitlyn winced at the nickname. Russ stepped toward her and enveloped her in a hug, and a twinge of jealousy pricked at Dev. Had Russ dated her before? Or was she one of the ones that Russ crudely categorized as *too good to screw with*?

"When did you get to town, Dev?" Alice asked.

"Today. I called Russ, and he spent the afternoon moving me from the Royal Grand Hotel to his condo."

"Well, of course!" Alice turned to Caitlyn. "These two were inseparable in college. It's been years since I've seen you, Dev. What gives?"

Dev smiled warmly at Alice. He'd always liked Russ's sparky little sister. "Right after college, Dad sucked me into the family business. After that it's been one thing after another. Thought I'd come to Royal to take a break from family drama." That was another thing he liked about Alice and Russ—while they may have their sibling spats, they were genuinely close and affectionate with each other. Their parents lived in Arizona and generally stayed out of their lives, but they supported Alice and Russ in whatever the duo wanted to do. Dev couldn't imagine his parents being so hands-off. As much as he loved his heritage, he envied the freedom Russ had to chart his own course.

His Indian parents interfered in everything, from what he ate for breakfast to what he wanted to do with his life. He'd just had a nuclear-level war with his family to come to Royal. He was looking forward to focusing on himself while he was here. It was time for him to pursue his own goals.

"He wants to open a restaurant here," Russ chimed in. "I'm going to help him."

"What type of restaurant?" It was the first time Caitlyn had spoken, and unlike Russ and Alice's Texas twang, she had the clean-cut accent of a finishing school graduate and a voice that was as sweet as a glass of perfectly chilled iced tea on a hot day.

It took him a second to remember what the question was. Russ slapped him on the back and jumped in. "Some hoity-toity fusion Indian cuisine. You should talk to Caitlyn—she's Royal upper crust."

Caitlyn narrowed her eyes, clearly not happy with the description. "We could use a nice Indian restaurant in this town." She gave him a warm smile, and a zing went through his body.

Alice handed the men a glass of wine each. "So, what're your plans?"

"I'm here for a month to scope out potential locations and do some market research. I understand there are already a lot of fine dining establishments here so I'll have to get to know the town to see whether there's room for another restaurant." His comment was for Alice, but he couldn't seem to take his eyes off Caitlyn. "Maybe a Royal native can give me a hand?" *Why waste an opportunity to mix business with pleasure?*

"Alice and I can take you around," Russ said affably, and Dev gave him an irritated look. Hadn't he brought Dev to entertain the friend? Then why was he butting in?

"Why don't we get dinner on the table? You guys were late, so the food is getting cold." Alice grabbed Russ's arm and took him to the kitchen.

A small smiled played on Caitlyn's lips, as if she was enjoying a private joke.

"What's so funny?" Dev whispered as he and Caitlyn stepped toward the dinner table. He needed to know what could bring such a beautiful smile to her kissable lips. Alice had pulled Russ into the kitchen, and they could hear furious whispering but not what was being said.

Caitlyn looked at him with mischief in her eyes, and heat licked deep in his belly. She lowered her voice. "If I had to guess, Alice is telling Russ right now that he needs to tell you to focus your attentions away from me. I'm supposed to be Russ's date tonight, although he doesn't know it."

Dev bit his lip so he didn't laugh out loud and catch Russ's attention. Caitlyn was staring at him, her eyes locked on his, and dancing with amusement. He bent his head and whispered in her ear, "Russ figured Alice would try to set him up, so he brought me here to entertain the friend." He caught a whiff of her fragrance, a muted vanilla and lavender. It was sweet and sexy and kicked up a fire deep in his belly.

He noticed a slight blush on her neck and ears and smiled.

"Ah, so you're his wingman." She took a tiny step away from him and sipped her wine.

"More like the distraction." He stood almost a foot taller than she, so he bent toward her to whisper, "Though I suspect that Russ has been trying to set me up with Alice for a bit now."

Caitlyn's smile dropped. "Would you like to go out with her?" Her voice was measured, but he heard the disappointment loud and clear.

"I've always seen Alice as Russ's little sister and therefore my little sister. I can't imagine dating her."

Her smile reappeared. "I agree completely. I've known Russ as Alice's brother, so it's hard to think of him romantically."

"So why did you come here tonight?"

Caitlyn sighed. "I need practice talking to men."

"Tell me you're kidding."

She shook her head. "I'm not good at making small talk and playing the dating game. Since Russ is exceptionally good at it, Alice thought it would be nice for me to practice with him."

He stepped closer, to see if she really was as skittish as she made herself sound, but she looked up at him, her eyes flirtatious, even challenging. *If this is what she calls shy, why isn't every man in Royal lining up to take her out?*

"So you were hoping to practice what, exactly, with him?"

Her neck and cheeks turned that delectable shade of pink, and he resisted the urge to place a hand on his heart.

"Just conversation. You know, flirting and small talk."

"Well, you don't seem to have any problems talking to me. Dare I say we're even flirting a little?"

She raised a brow. "Are you saying you're enjoying talking to me?"

He leaned in so his lips were almost touching her earlobe. She didn't back away, but he heard the sharp intake of her breath. "I'd like to do a lot more if you'd let me."

The pink in her cheeks deepened. "I mean talking, of course," he said cheekily. Though that was far from the truth. While he did want to talk to Caitlyn, what he really wanted was her alone to see exactly how pink her cheeks could get.

She took a long sip of her wine and gazed at him from under her lashes. Alice and Russ sounded like they were making their way back to the dining room with dinner. "You know what, you're right. I don't have trouble talking with you." She chewed on her lip and glanced toward the kitchen then back at him. "Can I ask you for a favor?"

Whatever you want, Caitlyn, you'll find me more than willing.

"I'm intrigued."

"Will you give me boyfriend lessons?"

Three

Caitlyn couldn't believe what had slipped out of her mouth. *Did I just ask a complete stranger to give me boyfriend lessons?* What was wrong with her? Had she had too much to drink? She looked down into her wineglass as if it would tell her how much she'd had. She calculated that she'd probably drunk a little more than two glasses. Not enough to blame her rash decision on alcohol.

It had been so easy to flirt with Dev, even for a short time. She'd never felt at ease with a date like that. With Dev, there was none of the paralyzing nervousness she felt when she met new men. She and Alice had just been talking about dating lessons, and then in walked a man she had no problem talking to, despite the fact that she was insanely attracted to him. If she could get comfortable with him, then she wouldn't have problems with other men. As a bonus, he was only in Royal for a month, so there was no chance that there would be awkwardness any time they saw each other in town. Nor would she have to avoid him like she'd had to avoid Jax over the past year.

Alice had arranged them around her rectangular dinner table so that Caitlyn was sitting across from Russ and next to Dev with Alice across from Dev. Alice had ordered a beef ragù ravioli in rosé sauce, steamed vegetables and garlic bread from the local Italian restaurant Caitlyn loved. It was a family favorite because of it's good food and unpretentious interior. Caitlyn had prepared a Caesar salad.

"This sauce is excellent," Dev said.

Russ scrunched up his nose. "I personally prefer the one from Primi Piatti. This one is too creamy."

"The creaminess comes from good-quality cheese. Most places just use cheap mozzarella." Dev scooped some sauce on his fork and licked it.

Caitlyn didn't want to stare, but she couldn't take her eyes off the way his tongue flicked out and licked the edge of the fork. A warmth pooled deep in her core, a feeling totally unexpected sitting at dinner. It usually took more than staring at a handsome stranger to get her going. A lot more!

"They also use Grana Padano in this sauce. That's what gives it the depth of flavor," Dev continued, and Caitlyn had to force herself to focus on what he was saying.

"You know your food," she said admiringly.

"In a different life, I would've been a chef."

"Why not in this one?"

Their eyes were locked together, and Russ and Alice faded from her consciousness.

He shrugged. "It's complicated. But that's why I'm opening a restaurant. I want to start a chain of high-end Indian fusion restaurants."

So he's Indian. Caitlyn had thought as much from his name. He was slightly darker skinned than she, but those green eyes—*oof.* His hair was thick and wavy and she wondered whether he'd like it if she ran her fingers through it.

"Why choose Royal for the first one?" Alice's voice broke through, and Caitlyn looked at her guiltily. She'd been completely focused on Dev beside her and had been ignoring Russ. Not that it mattered, because he seemed to be busy staring at his phone.

"Because Royal is far enough away from my family that they can't drop in on me. And from what Russ tells me, this town has the deep pockets and foodies to support a new restaurant. In a place like Vegas or LA, where new restaurants open every day, there won't be any buzz. I'd have to work ten times as hard to get attention. A town like Royal is full of wealthy—" While Caitlyn was studiously cutting a piece of ravioli into perfect square bites, she could feel his eyes on her. "—discerning individuals who appreciate fine dining."

Caitlyn looked up to see that he was indeed staring at her, a sparkle in his green eyes that sent her nerves tingling.

"Plus, the start-up costs in Royal are relatively low," Russ chimed in. "There are a number of places that went out of business in the heart of town, and their space is dirt cheap. I'm friends with the local Realtor. I'll set it up for you."

"Those businesses were lifelong Royal residents," Caitlyn said, irritated. "Mrs. Lowrey owned the little tea shop. It was passed down to her by her mother, who started it when she first moved to Royal in the 1920s. There's a hundred years of history that just got erased when they foreclosed."

"Russ didn't mean to sound so insensitive," Alice quickly jumped in. "Caitlyn tried to help those businesses get loans—even hosted charity events and got the wealthy ranchers to open their tight purse strings to help."

"What happened?" Dev asked, sounding genuinely interested.

Caitlyn shrugged. "We were able to keep several of the Main Street small businesses open, but a number of the older residents just didn't have it in them to keep going under the circumstances."

Dev smiled kindly. "You cared enough to do something about it. That counts for a lot."

"So, Russ, tell us, how is work going for you?" Alice said loudly, trying to get Russ's attention away from his phone.

Russ launched into a monologue of how he'd scored a major win. He worked as an investment banker, and while he was New York–based most of the time, he was back to take some "chillax" time.

Caitlyn found herself thinking about how she'd brazenly asked Dev to be her practice boyfriend, embarrassment mixing with anxiety and fear as the night went on. What must he think of her? She'd known him all of two minutes and had asked him to give her boyfriend lessons, like they were middle school children. Now that she had time to think, she wondered how best to extricate herself from the situation. Perhaps not mention it? Tell him she was joking? How could she even bring it up again?

When dinner finished, they all helped Alice pack up what was left of the food. Caitlyn was acutely aware of Dev moving around her in the dining room and kitchen. Alice took Russ to the kitchen to help her put away dinner—and probably to yell at him.

Caitlyn sat down in Alice's seat at the table so she was across from Dev. She didn't want to sit close to him again. All through dinner, she couldn't help glancing in his direction, and she hadn't missed Alice's glare every time she'd done it.

She took a sip of her wine, wondering where to start the conversation.

"So, how do I get in touch with my practice girlfriend?"

She clapped a hand on her mouth, but it was too late. The wine spluttered out of her mouth, across the table and onto his hand. She grabbed the napkin on the table and began mopping his hand and the table all at the same time, too mortified to even look at him. "Oh my God, I'm sorry. I'm so sorry."

He placed a hand on hers, stilling her frantic movements. She looked at him. There was a wide grin on his face, his eyes dazzlingly green. A warmth spread from her chest to her face. "I'm so sorry," she repeated in a small voice.

His hand was still on hers, and he stood and leaned over the table so his face was close to hers. Her entire body pulsed. His aftershave smelled like heaven, the scruffy five o'clock shadow on his jaw inviting her to rub her hands on it. "When we go out on our first date tomorrow, can you do that again? It's the sexiest thing I've ever seen."

She looked at him in horror. "I'm so sorry, it's a terrible habit."

He lifted his hand from hers and placed a finger on her lips as if to shush her. The feel of his finger made her lips tremble. He shook his head. "Don't ever be sorry for doing that again."

Alice cleared her throat, and both of them jumped back, as if they were teenagers caught by their parents.

"Dare I ask what's going on here?" Her voice was a little too high, and Caitlyn knew she was pissed.

"I did that thing I do when I get caught off guard while drinking wine," she said sheepishly, hoping to soothe the irritation etched on Alice's face. "Dev was helping me clean up."

Russ set down a stack of plates. "Uh-oh, you got the Caitie shower," he said. "We've all been victims."

Caitlyn wanted to crawl under the table and hide. Alice shot Russ a look. "Well, I have tiramisu for dessert, and Russ brought home a lovely ice wine that we opened."

Caitlyn wasn't hungry for dessert and wasn't sure she could stay much longer in Dev's company without incinerating and asking him to teach her more than just conversation. "I'm sorry, I have to leave. Since I knew I'd be drinking, I asked my brother to give me a ride, and he'll be heading home soon."

"Oh, stay. You can take an Uber later," Alice insisted, but Caitlyn shook her head. She was already planning to take an Uber—she'd used her brother as an excuse to make her escape.

Once Caitlyn had left, Russ decided it was time to play one of their old college games that involved a lot of drinking and a rehash of the most embarrassing/ frustrating moments of their lives. Alice wasn't too keen and neither was Dev, but Russ's exuberance was hard to ignore. After a while Alice held up her hands. "I think we're out of alcohol."

Russ booed her. "Guess it's time to call it a night."

"Before you do…" Alice turned to Russ. "What did you think of Caitlyn?"

Russ cocked his head. "Caitie? What's there to think about?"

Dev tried not to laugh. "Well, I thought she was fantastic."

Alice glared at him. "Caitlyn was supposed to be Russ's date."

Both men laughed, much to Alice's chagrin.

"Sis, you really should let me in on these plans of yours. Though I will admit Caitlyn isn't the shy little creature I remember. She's really come into her own."

Dev caught the note of interest in Russ's voice, and his heart seized. Was Russ interested in Caitlyn after all? If they'd been at a bar and interested in the same girl, they'd flip a coin. But this was different. Russ knew Caitlyn, and if he was interested in her, Dev couldn't stand in his way. Even though Caitlyn had seized his interest in a way he'd never experienced before. It wasn't just her stunning body or looks. Normally he couldn't stop thinking about what it would be like to take the woman to bed, but with Caitlyn, he'd been genuinely interested in getting to know her. There was something about her— perhaps it was the genuine innocence—that tugged at his heart strings. She seemed sincere and authentic, like she said what she meant and every sentence wasn't a calculated step toward some hidden goal. Russ wasn't the right man for her—he was a ruthless investment banker with a golden tongue when it came to lying to women to get what he wanted. Dev hated to think of Caitlyn, with her charmingly naive request for boyfriend practice, in Russ's hands. He shuddered. The man wouldn't think twice about taking advantage of her.

"So you interested in her?" he asked Russ more insistently than he'd intended.

"Dev, your tongue was hanging so far out of your

mouth, I'm surprised you weren't licking the plate instead of your lips," Russ said.

Dev punched him playfully but thought hard about his words. "Yeah, I think I like her—that's if you're not interested in her."

His heart stopped as he waited for Russ's reply, but Alice jumped in. "He is absolutely interested."

"Excuse me?" Russ glared at his sister, and Dev sat back. Even if Russ was interested in Caitlyn, there was no way he was going after her now and letting Alice win. Dev knew his friend well enough to know that Russ hated the way Alice interfered in his love life and how judgmental she was about the women he dated. Dev understood. His own family was constantly presenting the "biodata" of eligible Indian women from around the globe with the expectation that one of them would catch his attention. None had. Not like Caitlyn. At the thought of his family, a shiver went down his spine. They would never approve of Caitlyn. He shook the thought away. He wasn't marrying her. There was no reason to ever bring his family into their potential relationship.

Relationship? He'd just met the woman tonight. They hadn't even had sex and Dev was already contemplating a relationship? *One step at a time, Mallik*, he told himself.

The first step was getting Caitlyn's number from Alice.

"Alice, Russ isn't going to date Caitlyn because you're setting him up with her."

Alice glared at Dev, and Russ sat back in the

couch. "I'm goin' to let m' man Dev here have her," he said insolently, his Texas accent a little slurred.

"Neither one of you deserves her," she said icily. "I don't know what I was thinking, bringing her into this vipers' pit. That girl is way too good for either one of you. I'd hoped you—" she used her finger to stab Russ in the chest "—had grown up some."

Dev sat up and struck a more serious tone. "Seriously, Alice, I do really like her. She seems like a nice person, and I promise you I'll treat her well. Plus, she asked me to be her practice boyfriend, so I feel like I should at least text her to let her know I'm interested."

Alice's jaw dropped. Literally dropped. "She did what now? What else did she say?"

"Nothing. We didn't really get a chance to talk, what with you trying to insert Russ into the conversation. I don't even have her number to follow up and ask her out on a practice date. Any chance you'd share it?"

Alice narrowed her eyes, and he cringed at the ice-blue glare. "Not a chance. If I have anything to do with it, you aren't getting anywhere near Caitlyn."

Four

Caitlyn awoke the next morning to a text message from an unknown number on her phone. She threw back her comforter, groaning at how bright it was in her room.

When she returned home from Alice's house the night before, she'd found her family, minus Alexa, who was back in Miami, and the Grandins gathered in their living room. They were meeting to discuss their favorite topic: Heath Thurston's claim. They'd rehashed everything they knew, which wasn't much. The private eye had confirmed that Daniel was very likely Ashley's biological father, because the timing fit. But they still didn't know why Victor Grandin had given the oil rights to Cynthia and not to Ashley if it was supposed to be her birthright. Even more puzzling was why Augustus Lattimore had signed the papers. Jonas Shaw, the PI, was also working on finding out if the documents Heath Thurston had shared were legitimate.

Layla and Josh had been there as well, and Caitlyn had spent the entire night studying them surreptitiously, wondering if she'd share something like that with someone. Dev kept coming to mind, but she pushed the thought away.

After the Grandins left, her parents went to bed, but Jonathan, Jayden and Caitlyn stayed up talking. For once it was not about Caitlyn's dating life. None of them liked the idea of sitting around doing nothing while the PI did his work. Jonathan suggested they go through every single piece of paper that related to the property. Augustus, Ben's father and Caitlyn's grandfather, was so forgetful, even their father, Ben, couldn't be sure that he hadn't hidden something in the attic and forgotten about it.

Jonathan had hauled the boxes down from the attic. They'd already been through all the files in the study and Lattimore offices. It was time to unearth what had been hidden away. They had started going through the dusty, cobwebbed boxes. They found some interesting historical pictures, a lot of dead spiders and even a dead mouse in between some old books. They'd given up at the first light of dawn and Caitlyn had taken a quick shower to get the dust off, then crawled into bed.

She had several text messages from Alice but

ignored those. She needed to give Alice time to calm down.

Then she saw the text from an unknown number.

How's tonight for a practice date? Dev.

Dev? Had she given him her number? She rubbed her eyes and reread the text. His number wasn't saved in her contacts, so they hadn't exchanged numbers last night. Then she saw the texts from Alice.

Russ got your contact info from my phone and gave it to Dev.
Has he texted you?
DO NOT go out with him.
Call me when you see this.

She turned her attention back to Dev's text. What did he mean about a practice date? Her brain was a little foggy from the whiskey she'd shared with her siblings. It took a minute for last night's memory to make her sit up in bed, wide-awake. She'd asked a complete stranger for boyfriend lessons. *What have I done?*

She stared at the text message and her heart jumped. It had been so easy to talk to him, the usual feelings of dread and anxiety hadn't overtaken her. Then there was the image of Dev's green eyes, his tall frame, the way he'd licked that sauce off the fork. Warmth stirred deep in her core. She'd be crazy to go out with him. Surely there were better ways to practice her dating skills? She took a breath and typed out her response.

"So what exactly is a practice boyfriend?" Dev asked.

Caitlyn stopped before taking a sip of her water. How could she explain it to him when she hadn't been able to come up with an answer herself, despite having thought about it all day.

"Are you ready to order?" Caitlyn was grateful for the too-attentive waiter of the RCW Steakhouse, one of the fine dining restaurants in Royal. Dev had suggested it, and now he sat back in a collared shirt with the top button open and khakis. He looked effortlessly perfect—not too dressy, but not too casual.

Meanwhile, she'd shown up in her standard ladies' luncheon outfit—a knee-length pale pink sheath dress with a boat neck. She'd tried on every outfit in her closet. To ease the incessant fluttering that had taken hold in her belly ever since she'd texted Dev to accept his invitation, she'd chosen a familiar outfit. One that boosted her confidence and made her feel in charge.

"Tell me about the menu and specials." Dev asked the waiter with a healthy dose of amusement in his voice. The waiter launched into a description of each steak on the menu, finally ending with the special of the day, which was brisket.

"What do you recommend?" Dev turned to her.

"The steak," she quipped.

They both ordered French onion soup for an appetizer and prime rib for dinner, and then Dev let out a laugh. "Maybe I've been in New York too long, but steak houses there don't just serve steak. This is a really nice place but their menu could use some variety."

Caitlyn smiled. "This is a ranchin' town and RCW is a local favorite. I come here at least once a week."

"Does this town really need another fine dining restaurant?"

"It could." Caitlyn said quickly. "A lot of meetings and business gets conducted in restaurants. For example, the hospital board likes to come here for lunch. The women all order salads, minus the steak. They really come here for the whiskey. On that front, this place is the best in town, and if you want to attract the old ranchers, you need to make sure you offer premium alcohol at your restaurant."

He smiled and pretended to take notes. "Looks like you might be the one giving me lessons…on how to succeed in Royal."

Her cheeks warmed. What had come over her last night at Alice's? Maybe it was the wine, maybe it was the fact that she'd been unbelievably attracted to Dev. Or just some plain old crazy had come over her.

She went on to talk about wine, whiskey and bourbon, the drinks of the town. She wasn't usually this talkative, but she didn't want to go back to talking about what practice dating meant. The conversation flowed through dinner. Somehow, she didn't feel the tension that usually tightened her muscles on these dates. Dev's easy smile put her at ease.

"So what do you do?"

The dreaded question. There was no avoiding it. *Time for the spiel about all the important work I do to make it sound like I have a real job.*

She met his gaze and regretted doing so. His face was so open, his eyes warm and inviting. She remembered how he'd reacted when she'd spit her wine out at him. When that had happened with Jax, he'd made fun of her, repulsed like she'd thrown up on his good shoes. That's the way all men reacted. But not Dev.

She sighed. "I'm basically a socialite. As you gathered last night, my family is wealthy. After college, it was hard to focus on a job or career because my parents needed so much from me. Serving on the various boards that we get invited to, planning charity events, hosting events, etc. I'd be lying to you if I said that I was saving the world. I've just been untethered. I came back home after college and my family needed me, so I put my plans aside."

Every time a man found out that she didn't have a regular nine-to-five job, there were two types of responses—the guy either assumed that she wanted to live off her family money or that she was husband hunting. She couldn't decide which was more offensive. She searched Dev's face for which category he would fall into.

He reached out and put a hand on hers. The weight felt good on her hand, comforting. "Being there for your family is something to be proud of. Big families are complicated, and it takes an inordinate amount of work to keep people and business contacts on your side. Don't ever be apologetic for that."

Tears stung her eyes, and she blinked. "Do you also have a big family?" she managed to choke out.

He smiled. "I have big personalities in my family. I have one brother and one sister, both married with children. And parents who have a rather large business that they want me to take over, much to the discontent of my siblings."

She raised an eyebrow. She couldn't imagine fighting with her siblings for the family business. Part of the reason she took on so much of the family social work was because no one else wanted it, but it was an important part of keeping their standing in Royal and making sure that their ranching business got what it needed.

"Your siblings want the family business, but you don't want to give it to them?"

His lips tugged into a smirk as if the very idea was funny. He shook his head. "Ma and Dad grew up in India, where the eldest son takes over the family empire and takes care of the family. That's me. But I don't want to just inherit my father's wealth. I want to do something on my own, if only to prove that I can successfully run a business. That's why I'm in Royal. My siblings are more than happy to take over the family business, but they have a tendency to live lavish lives, and Dad is worried they'll run the business into the ground. He doesn't trust them, so I'm left playing the peacemaker between my father and siblings."

"Wow. So, what happens to your family business if you successfully launch your restaurant chain?"

"That is a question I refuse to think about. I'm hoping that me being out of New York for a month or so will give my sibs a chance to show Dad that they can step up. I love my father, but he's hard on all of us. Maybe if I'm not there, he'll see my sister's accomplishments. She really has a head for business, but my dad has refused to appreciate that."

Is this guy for real? Most men saw her attachment to her family and her constant focus on them as a sign of immaturity. But here was a guy who truly understood what it meant to love, care and sacrifice for his family.

"Are you going to miss your family while you're here?"

He shook his head and laughed. "I'm so done with family drama. Don't get me wrong, I would stand in front of a bullet for my family, but I need a mental break. That's why I chose Texas for my first restaurant. We have no businesses here, no reason for my family to appear. I need a break from family crises."

Caitlyn's heart fisted. She'd been about to share her own family's dilemma with him, but it was hardly fair.

"So, if you're done stalling with small talk, want to tell my why you need boyfriend lessons?"

No, I want to talk about anything but that.

He was looking at her with such a sparkle in his

eyes that her heart jumped and she lost the few words she'd formulated since the start of dinner. *Who asks such a gorgeous guy to be a practice boyfriend?*

"I find it hard to date." She swallowed, trying to get the words out of her dry mouth. "When I'm with a man, I get stiff and quiet. I need some practice dating, getting comfortable with small talk and flirting. You're the first one I've met who I didn't get all tongue-tied with. I didn't mean to spring it on you like that. I'd had a little too much to drink."

"Well, you haven't touched your wine tonight, and I don't see you having any trouble talking to me."

A fact that hadn't gotten unnoticed by her.

"Which is why you're the perfect guy to be a practice boyfriend. I'm comfortable with you and…" *Can tolerate the experience.* She stopped herself from saying the last part out loud. How could she explain to Dev the fear she felt every time she got close to a man? She couldn't even explain it to herself. *Cold fish.* Those were Jax's words but others had said a variation of them to her. The therapist she'd seen had called it a fear of intimacy. A fear that had come from what had happened with Jax.

The sex was fine, but it hadn't cured her inability to connect on an emotional level. She'd seen what Layla and Josh had, how they understood each other and the way they supported one another. Josh knew what Layla needed, and she intuitively took care of him. Was it too much to want the same thing?

He leaned forward. "So am I just meant for conversation or do we get to practice other things, too?"

A smile twitched on his lips, and while she tried to maintain eye contact, her heart skipped erratically. Her eyes involuntary dropped to his lips. They were so firm and lush. What would it be like to feel them pressing on the sensitive parts of her? Heat gushed deep in her core, and as she lifted her gaze and watched his eyes darken. She knew without a doubt that he could see what she was thinking.

We can practice anything you want. Wait, what? She broke eye contact and took a sip of her wine to do something other than think about him and her naked. She wanted to go out on dates, practice her conversational skills, learn how to get to know someone so she could connect with them emotionally. If she had sex with Dev, then their physical relationship would overshadow everything. She couldn't deny the attraction she felt to Dev, but what if she let things get physical and he also found her lacking? *No, that won't do. I have to make it clear to him that this is a platonic relationship.*

"Well, I was thinking I can keep you company as you do your research on the restaurants in town. I can show you around, introduce you to the movers and shakers, and in return you can teach me how to…"

"How to…?"

"Dessert?" Dev shot the waiter a dark look, but he didn't get the message, handing them the dessert menus. Caitlyn quickly declined dessert, and Dev followed suit. She didn't fully trust herself with him yet, it was best to end the date on a high note.

* * *

As Dev pulled out his wallet, Caitlyn waved to the waiter, pulling out her own credit card. "I should pay."

He shook his head. "Absolutely not. I invited you to dinner." When Alice had refused to give him Caitlyn's number, Dev had called in a favor with Russ to get her information. He hadn't been able stop thinking about her since last night. She was even more beautiful than he remembered from the night before. *Why would someone like her need a practice boyfriend?* Men should be falling over themselves to get a date with her. He'd just spent the last hour and a half enjoying talking about Royal, the history of Texas and foods from around the world. She was intelligent, witty and grounded. Not at all like the socialites he'd met in New York whose main focus was making sure they outdid each other, whether it was fashion, jewelry or Manhattan parties. She was the first woman he'd met in a long time whom he wanted to get to know, not just take back to his bed. Although *that* was something he also wanted to do. Eventually. As long as she was okay with the idea that their relationship was temporary. He had enough going on with his life that he wasn't interested in any type of long-term commitment. But while he hadn't planned on an affair in Royal, it would make his time here a lot more interesting.

"Yes, but you only invited me because I asked you to be a...practice boyfriend." She tripped over the last words, and he smiled.

As their server made his way over, Dev held out his card to the waiter, who plucked it out of his hand. "I asked you to dinner. Because I wanted to see you. Practice or not. Besides, this is a business expense, I'm here to check out the competition."

Caitlyn smiled widely, and he found himself smiling back, completely taken in by the sweetness in her eyes. "This place is a Royal institution. They'll be on of your main competitors."

"Russ has been telling me for years that there's no place like Royal to open a restaurant. Lots of deep pockets and a real appreciation for good food."

"He's right."

The waiter returned with the credit card receipt a little too efficiently. Dev was hoping to get some more time with Caitlyn. "Do you know a place where we can get coffee?"

She paused, and he was sure she was about to refuse him, but then she nodded.

As they walked out of the restaurant, he placed his hand at the small of her back. A gesture he hadn't even thought about until she stiffened. He removed his hand. *Did I do something wrong?*

They walked down the main street. The daytime heat had dissipated, so the night was warm but the slight breeze made it comfortable. The sun had set, but the last rays clung to the sky in hues of dark orange and purple. Old-timey streetlamps threw seductive shadows on the bricked sidewalk. It was the quintessential main street of old-town America. He longed to take her hand or tuck her arm in his, but he resisted. As they walked, she pointed out the various local businesses, most of which had closed for the day. He marveled at how she knew the names of each of the owners and their life stories.

She stopped in front of a red brick building with an old-fashioned sign that read General Store.

"Now if you are serious about opening a restaurant here, you need to make friends with Ol'Fred. Don't call him Fred. He likes to be called Ol'Fred."

"With the Texas twang?"

She smiled. "Yes. His family has been in Royal since the town was founded, and he not only knows all the landowners in town, anything you need to get things done, he's the man. He knows all the building contractors, the city inspectors and the permit architects at the county. And if you need a certain brand of tonic water for some spoiled brat cousin that even Amazon doesn't carry, he can get it for you."

They were standing underneath a streetlight, which emitted a soft golden glow on her face. He turned to face her, unable to take being so close to her and not touching her.

"Caitlyn, cards on the table. I like you. I want to spend more time with you, and not just because you can give me a crash course on all things Royal. What exactly do you want from me?"

She swallowed but didn't avert her gaze. "I don't want to be pitied because I usually can't get past a few dates. I want to learn how to open up to a man and have meaningful conversations, not just small talk. To connect on an emotional level."

He stepped closer to her. She stiffened but didn't step back.

"Is that all you want? To connect emotionally? What about physically, Caitlyn? Do you need practice with that?" His voice was low and thick, and he couldn't help it. She looked so devastatingly sexy and vulnerable that he wanted to—no, he *needed* to touch her, to let her know that she didn't need any help connecting with him, or anyone, for that matter. If she was having problems, the fault was clearly with the guy for not seeing the intelligent, caring person she was.

"I... I...don't know," she said helplessly. Her eyes darkened, and she dropped her gaze to his lips and her face tipped upward slightly.

"Then let me help you make up your mind."

He stepped closer and ran his hands down her bare arms, enjoying the soft, silky feel of her skin. He watched her face. She closed her eyes, and her lips parted slightly. Goose bumps sprang up on her arm, despite the hot night, and he knew she was feeling the same electric connection he was. He gently took her hand.

"Open your eyes."

She did.

"I'm going to kiss you now."

Her eyes widened. He bent his head and kissed her softly, just barely touching her lips, savoring the feel of her. He felt the slight pressure of her lips as she kissed him back and opened her mouth to him. He wanted more than anything to deepen the kiss, but he didn't want to scare her off. He put his arm around her waist to steady them. She felt so right pressed against him, and he couldn't help but pull her closer so he could feel the crush of her breasts against his chest.

That's when it happened. For the first time in his life, a woman pushed him away from her like she couldn't stand his touch.

Five

What have I done?

She hadn't meant to push him away so rudely. What she'd wanted to do was kiss him hard then untuck that stiff shirt and run her hands all over his chest. She'd pressed herself against him and felt the same heat that pulsed between her legs in his pants. And that scared the hell out of her. She didn't want to risk being rejected by him. *A cold fish.*

He stepped back from her and held his hands up. The streetlamp lit his eyes, which were filled with horror. "I'm sorry I misread things, Caitlyn. I didn't mean to kiss you if you didn't want it."

Didn't want it? That's not the problem. She wanted it *too much*, with a fire and intensity that didn't make any sense. It was just a kiss. He was just a guy.

She shook her head. "No, I'm sorry. I didn't mean to do that."

"Kiss me or push me away?"

Both.

"Push you away. I don't know what came over me. I've never done anything like that before."

"Am I so bad a kisser?" he said lightly, placing a hand on his chest where she'd pushed him. He looked so devastatingly, boyishly handsome, her heart fisted. She'd expected him to get angry, to yell at her, utter some expletives. She had wanted the kiss. He had warned her that he was about to kiss her. She wanted to lie to him and tell him that she'd changed her mind about him being a practice boyfriend. That she didn't want to see him anymore. This non-relationship was already too intense.

But isn't that exactly what I want?

"It's the opposite problem, actually. It was just so… good."

"Now, that's a more interesting answer." He stepped closer to her. "What do you mean?"

"Do you mind if we walk?" It was too disconcerting, having him looking at her. As irrational as it was, she couldn't help feeling he could read her thoughts. She didn't want him to know how out of control he made her feel.

"Lead the way."

As they walked down the main town street, she resumed her informational session on Royal businesses. She was avoiding the conversation. She knew it, and Dev knew it, but he let her go on, asking her questions about Royal and about her family. Familiar, comfortable topics. When they reached the tack shop, she stopped.

"This is where everyone in town buys their fancy equestrian items for the horses they ride in shows."

"Do you ride?"

She nodded and looked wistfully at the shop. Dev was in town pursuing his dream, and yet hers was stalled.

"What is it?"

She turned to him in surprise. "Nothing."

He rolled his eyes. "I have a sister and a mother, so I know when a woman says 'nothing' it really means 'everything.'"

Now it was her turn to roll her eyes. "Oh, please, don't mansplain me. Sometimes it also means I don't want to talk about it, or more importantly, I don't want to talk about it with *you*."

He smiled. "C'mon, I'm your practice boyfriend. If you can't tell me, then who?"

The laughter in his voice was infectious, and it made her smile at her own ridiculousness. "Fine, if you must know. I have this plan—more of a dream, actually—of starting a horse-riding program for foster children on the Lattimore ranch. I've been around horses all my life, and it's been an amazing experience for me and a teaching tool in how to care for an animal, how to feel one with another living being."

She pointed to a belt buckle in the shop. It was

a big silver buckle studded with rhinestones. "That buckle costs what most foster families make in a month. They can't afford to send kids to horse riding camps. We have all these horses that we hire staff to ride because no one has the time to groom and ride them. Seems like such a waste."

"So what's stopping you?"

"I can't just open up the Lattimore ranch and ask kids to come on over and ride horses. I have to get permits, inspections—it's a whole process."

He raised an eyebrow. "I get it. You pissed off Ol'Fred and he's standing in your way."

She smiled. "Ol'Fred has been offering to adopt me since I was a little girl. He'd do anything to help me."

"So then?"

"It's just life. I have all these obligations and board commitments. It's hard to find the time."

"Sounds like excuses to me."

"What?" *How dare he?* He didn't have any idea what her life was like.

He turned to face her. The light from the tack shop threw shadows across his face. He raised his hands like he was going to touch her, then crossed them. "You seem like the type of woman who knows how to get things done in this town. If you want to open this camp, I bet you could make it happen with a snap of your fingers. So, what are you waiting for? What's stopping you? The real reason, not the one you're telling yourself and everyone else."

She wanted to give him an angry response, but

the warm look in his eyes and the crease on his forehead melted her heart. She was looking for genuine connection. What had her therapist said? That she put up blocks, hid behind her conversation talking points. Normally her dates didn't care to probe past what she said. They were too focused on how the night would end and whether she'd accept an invitation to their bed. But Dev wanted to know more. He wanted to talk about things she hadn't prepared for.

She swallowed, then looked into the tack shop window to avoid his gaze. "I'm the youngest in the family. I have two brothers and a sister. They've looked out for me my whole life. Made sure I'm successful in whatever I do."

"You've never done anything on your own."

She shook her head. "It's not that. I've planned many charitable events and social programs. You're right. I can do this in my sleep. But I've never done anything this important. Since the pandemic, the foster program has been overwhelmed. And it's not just the stories you expect—kids who are abandoned, abused or neglected. It's kids whose parents love them but lost their jobs and couldn't make ends meet. The state forcibly took the kids because they were living in cars and homeless shelters. Neither the parents nor the kids want to be apart, but the state has to put the kids in a stable home. Then there are cutbacks to the state program so the families who foster get little support and are overwhelmed themselves. These kids are moved from one family to another. And even when the kids find a good family, they feel they have to be loyal to their birth parents and don't know how to process the emotions they feel toward their foster parents."

Tears sprang to her eyes as she thought about the kids she'd met. She volunteered at the child protection services office, babysitting kids who were waiting for placement. Playing with them and giving them the attention that the social workers who were busy finding them families didn't have the bandwidth for.

"I want to give them something that's stable. A place where they feel safe and can connect with a living being without the complications of a label like 'foster dad' and 'real mom.'"

"Is that how you feel about horses?"

She startled. "What?"

"A horse only needs water, food, shelter and grooming. No complicated human emotions with horses."

A bitter taste swirled in the back of her throat. Was that why she'd always gotten along with horses? Because they didn't expect any real feelings from her? No, that couldn't be true. She loved her horses, talked to them, bonded with them. They sensed when she was sad or angry. But they didn't expect as much from her as a man, that much was true. Yet she wasn't about to admit that to Dev. They'd already gotten a little too close for comfort.

She sighed. "Horses sense feelings and emotions. They need love, which is why a riding program for kids is so perfect. They have so much love to give, and they just don't know where to direct it some-times."

He bent his knees so he was face-to-face with her, forcing her to look at him. His eyes were soft, even a little shiny. "You are a wonderful person, Caitlyn. I hope you know that. To care about something other than yourself is something very few people know how to do."

Then why am I such a cold fish? she almost blurted out. She tried to smile at him, but tears threatened to spill out of her eyes, so she turned her gaze back to the tack shop window. "I was ready to start my program, but there's an issue with my ranch. I don't want to start the program and have to take it away."

"What do you mean?"

Could she tell him? "It's exactly the type of fam-ily drama you don't want to get involved in."

He laughed now. "As long as it's not *my* family drama, I don't care. C'mon, spill it."

She told him about Heath Thurston's claim.

"Let me get this straight. Ashley might be the blood relative, but Cynthia is Ashley's mother, and the oil rights were given to her."

"Correct, which actually makes the claim stron-ger, because Heath and Nolan are Cynthia's sons, so they directly inherit from their mother. But there are still some things that don't make sense, so we've hired a PI to find out."

"I'm sorry, I'm not a rancher. Why does Victor Grandin, is it?" She nodded, so he went on. "Why does he get to give the oil rights to your land to cover up his son's sins?"

"That's the baffling part. My grandfather signed the papers so the rights beneath our land are included."

"Didn't you say you live with your grandfather? Why not ask him?"

"Augustus is ninety-six years old and has memory issues. We've tried asking him, and each time we get a different story. We're trying to find out whether the signature is even genuine."

"So how does this affect your horse camp?"

"If the claim is real, and Heath and Nolan Thurston decide to exercise their rights, they'd be digging wells right where the stables are. We'd lose the stables and horses. I can't do that to those kids. While all this could take some time, I can't let them fall in love with something that then gets yanked away from them."

"Is that what happened to you?"

"What?"

"Is there something that got taken away from you?" he asked softly.

Her heart beat wildly in her chest, and her palms felt greasy. She was the most privileged child she knew. A biracial baby adopted by a wealthy, loving family who doted on her. There was absolutely nothing that she could have asked for in her life that hadn't been handed to her. The only thing she'd ever lost was Jax, her high school best friend and perhaps the love of her life.

She shook her head. "I'm the story every foster kid dreams of. My parents adopted me when I was a baby. My family, including my siblings, love me like crazy. I couldn't ask for anything in my life."

"Does that make you feel guilty?"

"What?"

"That you were given a chance with your family that the foster kids don't have? Is that why you want to open the horse ranch?"

She took a shuddering breath. *How did he know?*

"It's okay to feel guilty, for having it all, you know. To even feel resentful for it. You didn't ask for it."

This time she didn't stop the tears that squeezed out of her eyes. All her life, she'd been told how lucky she was, to be grateful for the gift she'd been given. That's why she'd returned home after college to take over the Lattimores' charitable and community work. To give back a little bit of what she'd gotten. Yet all she felt was guilty. For having it all. For not giving back enough. For not saving all the other kids, the majority of them Black, from the fate the Lattimores had saved her from.

Dev lightly placed a hand on her arm then extended his other arm, inviting her to step into his embrace. She couldn't resist. Stepping close, she placed her cheek against his chest and immediately felt his warmth strengthen her.

You know Royal has a ghetto? It's where people like me live. Where your butler, gardener, cook and Ol'Fred live. Jax had said those words to her when he'd gone off to college. It was his way of telling her there was a whole world she needed to see. The real world. He hadn't said it with malice, but it still hurt.

Dev was almost a foot taller than she was, even with her heels. Yet she fit perfectly against him. She focused on the beating of his heart, which seemed to be racing as wildly as hers. Closing her eyes against the rise and fall of his chest, she took deep breaths to push Jax out of her mind. Here was a man who wasn't obliged to be with her. He was here because he wanted to be. No one was forcing him.

"How about we make a deal?"

Caitlyn stepped back from Dev, blinking away the remaining tears in her eyes.

His green eyes sparkled. "How about I agree to be your practice boyfriend and help you figure out how to make your horse camp happen, and you introduce me around town and help me set up my restaurant?"

She smiled. "What exactly does being a practice girlfriend entail?"

He grinned. "I like how you turned this around on me."

While she'd pulled back from his embrace, his hands were still loosely on her arms, and she liked them there, liked the weight of his touch, the slight smell of soap and aftershave. Maybe it wouldn't be that bad an idea for him to be a full boyfriend. What if she slept with him? What's the worst that could happen? Their relationship would end the same way her others had? So what? Dev was only going to be in Royal for a month. He'd told her at dinner that he planned to open the restaurant, then return to New York to his family business before continuing to establish a chain of restaurants. He wasn't planning on living in Royal. He wasn't going to be a long-term anything, and she planned to be a lifelong Royal. If along the way he could help her get more comfortable with men, that's all she needed. Wasn't that the point of boyfriend lessons anyway?

"Here's what I can offer you as a practice boyfriend," Dev said, and Caitlyn followed the smooth, thick sound of his voice, letting herself get pulled in. He was a man—he would ask for the thing all men wanted. And she was ready to say yes.

"We can spend time together, go out on dates and get all the conversation time you want."

She nodded, waiting for the next part. Because suddenly, that's the part she really wanted.

"I'm not going to touch you without your permission. And I'm not going to sleep with you."

"Wait, what?" She hadn't meant to say that out loud. It had been in her head but had come out most unexpectedly.

He smiled. "I've never had to entice a woman into my bed, and I'm not going to start now. We'll keep it a platonic relationship, unless…"

Her throat closed. "Unless?"

He leaned over, his lips oh so close to hers but not quite touching. "There's a lot more that I can teach you other than conversational skills." She sucked in a breath, wanting desperately to move an inch forward and press her lips on his. But he seemed to be moving away.

"But if you want more, you're the one who's going to have to seduce me."

Six

She sat up, hot and sweating, in her own room with its pastel-blue ceiling and soft gray walls. She'd been dreaming about Dev giving her lessons in bed. The kind of lessons that made her breathing heavy, her body sweaty, and matted her hair to her head. Caitlyn rarely dreamed, but when she did, they were vivid and visceral. But this dream was crazy. It didn't take a genius to figure out what it all meant.

As if he could sense her thinking about him, her phone buzzed with a text from him.

Going to check out a restaurant on Colton Street at 9 am. Are you free to come with me? Practice brunch date afterward?

It had been less than twelve hours since she'd seen him, but the idea of going out with him filled her with excitement. She texted him back then sprang out of bed. With only forty-five minutes to get dressed, she wouldn't have time to wash her hair, which was a bit of a production. She did a quick conditioner wash to get the sweat out, then pulled it back into a ponytail, forgoing perfectly straight hair that she usually re-curled into perfect waves. Her hair was naturally curly, but not the tight curls or long locks Alexa had. She often envied her sister's perfect hair.

She chose a sundress, one of her favorites that she usually wore around the house, a peacock-blue dress that wrapped around her with a deep V-neck and a hemline that ended right before her knees. Her smart watch told her the day would be hot, so she knew better than to wear makeup. It would just melt and make her face look splotchy. Plus, she didn't have much time, so she settled for a swipe of lip gloss and threw on strappy but flat sandals in case there was a lot of walking to do.

She took one last look in the ornate full-length mirror in her walk-in closet and had to admit that she liked this new look. If she didn't know better, she'd say she looked like one of those flirty girls on the cover of a fashion magazine. She normally dressed so businesslike. Her hair was always perfectly pressed and styled, never in natural curls, as it was now with nothing but a scrunchie. Caitlyn wasn't vain, but she knew that she was generally a beautiful woman, having been blessed with big eyes, a small, straight nose and lips that fit her face perfectly. Her skin color ranged from a beige to a golden brown, depending on her summer tan. Looking at the bottles of different-colored foundations on her dresser, she quickly took an extra minute to put on sunblock. She had a series of Royal events on her calendar where it would definitely not be suitable to show up without makeup or with wild hair. But the morning belonged to Dev.

Dev had offered to pick her up, but she chose to drive into town. Against her father's wishes, she'd opted for a Tesla Model 3. It was dwarfed on the road and in her driveway by the bigger cars, but she liked the electric car among the gas guzzlers in town. It was Sunday, so she didn't have any meetings, but she did want to stop by the child protection services office to see if they needed her help later in the day. They'd been short-staffed lately, and she often found the social workers there on Sundays. She helped them with filing or photocopying so they didn't spend their entire Sunday working.

She arrived five minutes late. Dev had asked her to meet him inside the restaurant, but he was waiting by the door for her. She pulled to the curb. He had been leaning against the brick wall of the building, one leg bent, his eyes on his phone. He wore a V-neck T-shirt and jeans. His hair looked perfectly mussed, with soft waves that kissed his brow. He looked up when she arrived.

"That's not a legal spot. There's a parking lot in

the back." He gestured to the little driveway a few feet away.

"I know. But don't worry, I won't get ticketed. Sorry I'm late."

He came around the front of the car as she collected her purse and opened the door. Or tried to. It was locked. He grinned, and she unlocked it. When it clicked, he tugged again.

"These car manufacturers make it really hard to be chivalrous."

"That's because chivalry is dead. Instead, those gentlemen of yesteryear are replaced by creeps that try to carjack and assault women, which is why car doors automatically lock."

He shook his head as he extended his hand to help her out of the car. She didn't need help but liked it. It gave her an excuse to touch him.

As she brushed past him, he whispered, "You look amazing, by the way." She warmed, not at the compliment but by the thickness in his voice as he said it.

He let go of her hand, then held his out. She looked at him, confused.

"Am I supposed to give you something?"

He smiled. "Your car keys, so I can park it in the lot."

She laughed. "Actually, this car has no keys. It runs off the app on my phone. Is that what women in New York do? Hand you their keys and say 'park the car'?"

"Not exactly, but they are used to a certain amount of male chivalry."

She shook her head. "My car is fine here. I know the cops on the parking beat—they never ticket my car."

His eyebrows rose. "Well, don't you have the town of Royal wrapped around your little finger."

"It's amazing how much appreciation a few charity events, and bagel and coffee at the precinct buys you."

He did a mini bow. "You are truly the princess of Royal."

The door opened, and a man in a suit stepped out of the restaurant. He was tall, lanky, with sandy blond hair and blue eyes. He smiled widely as he saw her. "Miss Caitlyn, I had no idea you were the friend Mr. Mallik said we were waiting for."

"Greg, it's so nice to see you," Caitlyn said genuinely. "It has to have been over a year since you were last at the ranch. Your dad told me you'd gone into commercial real estate."

He nodded proudly. "And doin' real well, thanks to Mr. Lattimore's recommendations, miss."

"Greg, we're the same age, please call me Caitlyn."

Dev looked at Caitlyn. "How do you two know each other?"

"We live in the same town—a lot of us know each other."

Greg piped up, "She's bein' too kind. My daddy works as a ranch hand on the Lattimore estate. I grew up workin' every summer at Miss Caitlyn's."

"Greg, please call me Caitlyn."

He turned slightly red at her second request, seeming unsure whether it would be more offensive to heed her request or undo his very traditional father's strict request to call everyone up at the mansion by Mr. or Miss or Mrs.

"Let me show you the place. It used to be…"

"…the old Stevens brewery," Caitlyn finished.

Greg nodded. "Miss…sorry, Caitlyn here knows more about Royal history than anyone. Well, except Ol'Fred."

Caitlyn realized that she was interfering with Greg's carefully planned spiel, so she deferred to him to tell the rest as Greg showed them the space. The brewery had been closed for almost a decade. The Stevenses had been an old couple who ran it for nearly thirty years. When they died, they left the brewery to a nephew who lived in Los Angeles, and he put it up for sale. It had changed hands a couple of times—a local rancher tried to open up a steak house, which competed with the RCW Steakhouse and it became a town feud. The rancher gave up on it and sold the property to a chain restaurant. It didn't do very well. The leftovers of the red icon still hung over the old wood bar. The place was in rough shape, having been on the market for several years with little maintenance. Someone had swept up recently, but the old wooden floors were caked with mud and dirt, and the stale smell of old water, dead mice and long-ago yeast still hung in the air.

Dev asked Greg several questions about the sale terms and the condition of the kitchen equipment.

Greg had done his homework, and Caitlyn made a note to tell his dad just how well he was doing. She knew Mr. Hodges was always tough with him. Caitlyn hadn't really known Greg when they were growing up, even though she visited the stables daily. *You never socialize with those who aren't in your stratosphere.* Jax had said that to her when he had first returned home from college. At the time he'd said it with a laugh but she later learned that he'd meant those words.

"How about I leave you two to discuss it? I'll just be two doors down at the café when you're done. Let me know and I'll lock up," Greg said, smiling.

Dev turned to Caitlyn once Greg had left. "If I didn't know better, I'd say the lad was crushing on you."

Caitlyn frowned. "What? No! Greg's just…he's Greg."

"Greg is an all-American male, and he has a crush on young Miss Caitlyn." Dev added Greg's accent when he said her name, and she laughed.

"So what you do think of the place?"

They stood in the center of what was supposed to be the dining room. Caitlyn had never been in this place before, but she'd heard about it from the locals when it was the brewery.

Dev was deep in thought. "It's nice. It certainly has good bones and old-world charm, but it's just so…"

"Just so…"

Dev clicked his fingers as if trying to find the words.

"… Texas," Caitlyn supplied.

He grinned. "Yes. Exactly. Like the RCW Steakhouse."

"It's the kind of place old men would come to eat bloody steak and smoke cigars."

They both laughed at that. "I need my place to feel like you're coming to eat at a relative's house. It's different, it's not everyday, but it's homey."

"And you're looking for that in Royal?"

"Would you eat in a place like that?"

She nodded, acknowledging the trap. "I think the younger generation of Royal is not quite as big on stuffy and formal restaurants. They are well traveled and appreciate new and refined cuisine."

Dev nodded. "Well, this is the first of three places Russ had prioritized for me to see. Let's hope the other ones are better."

"You'll find something," Caitlyn said reassuringly.

They looked at each other for a moment. "I really like this look on you," he said.

"What look is that?"

His lips twitched. "This natural look, like you don't have a care in the world."

"This Caitlyn usually doesn't step out of the house."

"Why not?"

Why not indeed? She shrugged. "I just feel like it's an expectation, you know. I'm a Lattimore, and

I need to represent the family." Even as she said the words, she knew they weren't true. Her parents had never put any pressure or expectations on her, and her siblings certainly didn't act that way.

"Are you sure it's not body armor?"

"What would I need body armor for? I have everything I could possibly ask for." She didn't like the pitch of her voice when she said those words, even though they were true.

"Well, I like all your looks, Caitlyn, but this is definitely my favorite." He stepped closer to her, and she felt a slight tug as he wrapped one of her curls around his finger.

"I like your hair natural."

He was close to her, and she breathed in the spicy scent of his aftershave. It was seductively woodsy. Why did she want a platonic relationship again? He was nearly a foot taller than her, so she was looking up and noticed a tiny shaving cut on the side of this jaw. She touched her finger to the cut, and he froze, then stepped back from her.

"Wait, you got to touch mine, but I don't get to touch yours?" she said playfully, marveling at the seduction that had naturally crept into her voice. It was as if she was someone else entirely. His green eyes darkened, and her insides melted.

She lifted her fingers and touched his hair. He sucked in a breath, and she smiled, feeling a surge of excitement. His hair was soft, not textured like hers, but thick and naturally wavy. He didn't use a lot of hair product. She liked that. What would it be like to run all her fingers into his hair and tug? Would he like it?

He cleared his throat. "Are you done fondling my hair?"

She retreated her hand and stepped back several paces suddenly embarrassed at the naked lust that she was sure was written all over her face.

He closed the distance between them. "Caitlyn, don't get me wrong. I want you to touch my hair. I want you to touch a lot more than my hair." His voice was low and thick and his eyes dark pools of molten heat. Her own skin was enticingly warm and tingly. "I'm doing my best to be a gentleman here, but know this…" He bent a little closer so his lips were mere inches from hers. His breath was so close to her mouth that she wanted to suck it in. "…anytime, anyplace you want me, you can have me. No questions asked."

She did suck in that breath, unsure of what to say or how to react. Deep inside, a voice screamed, *Take me now, put me against the bar, lift up my skirt and show me just how much you want me.* But that voice stuck in her throat. He waited for what seemed like an eternity, then straightened and stepped back from her. The silence stretched between them until he broke it. "I guess Greg is waiting for us. Let's give him the keys and I'll take you to brunch."

She nodded and followed him out, knowing the moment was lost and wondering if she was falling into the same old patterns again.

Seven

"This could be the set for a horror movie," Caitlyn said.

They were sitting in Dev's rental car waiting for Greg to show up. It was early in the morning, but the place they were visiting was clearly deserted. They had unbuckled their safety belts but felt it best to wait for Greg before they went exploring. The structure before them looked like it had been a diner once. The large neon sign had stopped working, but the letters were visible. The windows were large, and beyond the coat of dust and grime, they could barely make out gingham curtains. The parking lot was spacious, with no spaces for handicapped parking, indicating the place had been closed a very long time.

"I think Russ is purposely setting me up with

these terrible properties to punish me for moving out to the hotel."

"Was he mad?" Caitlyn asked.

Dev nodded. "He took it as a personal affront to his hospitality. Never mind that the guy's idea of breakfast is still Froot Loops, 'cowboy style,' as he calls it, meaning dry, because it's too much to keep fresh milk in the fridge."

"You should do something to make nice with him."

Dev nodded. "I promised him we'd go out one night. Apparently, there's some Lone Ranger night-club that he's dying to take me to."

Caitlyn felt an irrational bubble of anger. "The Lone *Star* is a meat market. It's where singles go to hook up."

Dev looked at her, his green eyes mischievous. "Would it bother you for me to go there?"

Caitlyn looked toward the diner so he wouldn't see her eyes. He had an uncanny way of reading her. It had been two weeks since the first night they'd met and she had seen Dev almost every day, either to look at a property with him when her time allowed, or at dinner. They were almost in a routine. He texted her each morning asking what her day looked like then suggested a way for them to see each other. Yesterday she'd been tied up all day, so they'd met for coffee in between her afternoon meeting and her dinner charity event at the Texas Cattleman's Club. Caitlyn had wrangled with whether to invite Dev as her date rather than showing up alone yet again, but she had ultimately decided against it. There would be too many questions—ones she wasn't ready to answer yet. She didn't need any more gossip among the Royal residents. They still asked her about what happened with Jax and they'd broken up a year ago.

Jax. The other reason she hadn't invited Dev to the gala last night. She hadn't known if Jax would be there. On the off chance he would, she wanted to face him alone. They hadn't seen each other since *that* night, but she knew it was time for them to talk. They'd spent too long avoiding each other. In an odd way, spending time with Dev made her less nervous about the difficult conversation that lay ahead with Jax.

Despite the sexual tension that simmered between them, it was easy to talk to Dev. Maybe it was that he didn't let her get away with canned answers. He always pried and probed until she felt coaxed into talking. She'd shared more of herself with Dev in two weeks than she had with any other man. Even Jax. She knew Dev was only here temporarily, but she didn't want to share him with someone else, even for one night.

"What would you do if I said I don't want you to go?"

He didn't answer, so she looked at him. He was staring at her. Since the day in the old Stevens brewery, their time together had been physically distant. While she enjoyed spending time with him, she was reminded of her physical attraction to him and could no longer ignore the sexual frustration she felt.

"Why don't you want me to go, Caitlyn?"

The ball was in her court. She understood that. But she couldn't help fearing what would happen if she took the next step. She'd never had such an easy rapport with any man. They flirted, laughed, shared deeply personal thoughts, and she finally understood what her therapist meant about her needing to open up. She didn't want to lose that. What if they slept together and it didn't work out? As it is, there were a scant two weeks before he left Royal. Maybe friendship was all she should take from him.

"I don't want us to practice anymore. I want to be with you, physically." The words tumbled out of her before she could stop them. His darkening eyes mesmerized her and she leaned forward. He didn't hesitate, and closed the distance between them. His hand cupped her cheek, and he pressed his lips firmly to hers. His tongue flicked across her bottom lip, and she lost all rational thought. Her entire body quivered, her core hot and desperate for his touch. This time she didn't hold back. She let her tongue tangle with his. When the kiss wasn't enough, she twisted her body and tucked a knee underneath her so she could get even closer to him.

The kiss broke and she moaned in protest, but Dev pulled back and cleared his throat. "Greg is here."

She noticed him adjusting his pants, and she looked down to see that her wraparound dress was twisted so her ample cleavage was on full display. She didn't miss Dev's appreciative glance but sat back in the seat and quickly adjusted her dress.

Greg tapped on the window, and Dev and Caitlyn looked at each other and smiled.

The diner was in such rough shape that they couldn't really go inside. When Greg unlocked the door with a set of old-fashioned keys, the lock was so rusted that he had to force the handle, which in turn led to the door splintering on its hinges. The wooden flooring inside had significant cracks, and none of them felt like testing whether it could hold their weight.

Greg smiled apologetically. "As I said, the property is in rough shape, but there are really no more options on the west side of Royal. This is at the very edge. I know this building would have to be a tear-down, but this property comes with fifty acres of land and a barn that's in usable shape."

Dev's eyebrows shot up. "Fifty as in five zero."

Greg nodded, and Caitlyn had the urge to giggle at Dev's wide eyes.

"This is Texas, darlin'. That kind of land is not uncommon." She smirked.

"Yeah, I'm used to New York properties, where we talk in inches, not acres."

"It's a pretty nice parcel of land—flat, clear lot. I know the ladies' auxiliary has been rentin' it regularly for their clothing drives."

"That barn has an entrance through *Piedmont Road* right?" Caitlyn confirmed.

Greg nodded. "But you see that little footpath there?" He pointed to the other side of the parking lot. "That'll lead you right through the trees and to the barn. You might want to go see it since you're already here."

Caitlyn turned to Dev. "I've been in that barn once. It's actually pretty nice. Maybe the restaurant can be situated there."

Dev raised his brow. "Really?"

"No harm in checking it out," Caitlyn said.

"Well, you folks go ahead. I'm gonna have to do some callin' around, see who I can get to come board up that door," Greg said. "It won't be right to leave it like that." He handed them a set of keys. "These will open the side entrance. Drop them off in town at the real estate office when you're done. Now you be careful walkin' around."

Dev still looked skeptical, but Caitlyn grabbed his hand. "C'mon."

She took him out back. Thick shrubbery overwhelmed the narrow footpath. "Are you sure about this?" He looked pointedly towards her bare legs and sandaled feet.

She nodded. An idea had come to her when Greg mentioned the barn, but she wasn't sure Dev would understand it until he saw the space.

She led him through the thicket of trees, and they emerged in a field that had long ago browned and dried up. A large red barn stood about two football fields away.

"Wow, that looks like it could be on the cover of *Farm and Country.*"

Caitlyn was pleased that the barn was the one she remembered. From the outside, it looked like a quintessential farm barn—tall with a sloping gray roof and white cross-hatched windows. The once-red paint was now a dull maroon, and as they got closer, they could see that the wood siding on the barn was cracked and peeling in several places. They walked around to the side, past the big front doors, as Greg had instructed, and to a side entrance. They unlocked the padlock, and the door opened easily.

Inside, the cavernous space smelled like earth and pine cones. It must have been recently used, because rubber pavers had been added to the floor, and several six-foot tables were set up in the center of the room. There were a number of cardboard boxes here and there but overall, the space was neat. The artificial pine cone smell came from several tree-shaped air fresheners that had been hung across the wooden slats delineating the hayloft. Caitlyn smiled. Only the ladies' auxiliary would try to freshen up a barn. She walked over to the double front doors and deftly unlocked them from the inside, throwing them open and bathing the barn in sunshine and fresh air.

"So, I have a crazy idea."

Dev smiled, "I can't wait to hear it." There was no snark in his voice, just pure interest, and she tried not to notice how alluring his emerald green eyes shone in the sunlit barn. There was no doubt in her mind that he was more interested in picking up where they left off in the car. Not that she wasn't. The barn was deserted, after all, and oddly romantic.

"This town has plenty of upscale restaurants. What if you opened a family Indian fusion restaurant? Imagine dining tables inside where parents can sit and enjoy a nice meal. And outside, you set up a playground where the kids can run around, get some fresh air. You can even have an indoor-outdoor kitchen. Build a tandoori oven outside where your chef can bake fresh naan."

"Someone's been doing their homework on Indian cuisine."

She smiled shyly. She had been doing a lot of research, but she wasn't about to admit just how much time she'd spent trying to learn a little more about his culture. She'd learned that *chai* meant tea, so saying "chai tea" was redundant. Just like *naan* meant bread, so saying "naan bread" was the same thing. She'd realized that he spent so much time asking about her that she hadn't learned much about his heritage from him.

"I like the concept, but to renovate this space will require a lot of resources. I was banking on creating a luxury brand. I don't see the clientele from RCW Steakhouse, or a lot of the ranchers in this town, sitting down to eat in a barn. In New York, yes, people would drive hours to have this type of experience, but not here. They'd feel like they were in their own backyard. I think upscale is the way to go."

He wasn't wrong on that front, and her heart deflated.

"Hey, what's wrong?" He stepped toward her and bent down so he could look her straight in the eyes. How was Dev such a mind reader? She shook her head, not trusting herself to speak.

"It's written all over your face." He placed his hands on her bare shoulders, and his touch heated her insides.

"I guess I want you to find a space here in Royal so you don't leave."

He smiled. "You're enjoying my company that much, huh?"

She lifted her face so she could meet his gaze. She ran her fingers along his jawbone, then across his bottom lip. His lips parted, and she grabbed his chin and pulled him toward her. Their lips crashed, and every single second she'd spent holding herself back from being with him destroyed the last threads of inhibition still holding her together.

She wrapped her arms around his neck and pulled him closer, pressing her body to his. With her flat sandals, she had to go on tiptoes even with his head bent. She fit perfectly into him, and just as she felt the hot heat between her legs, his erection pressed hard into her belly. His hands went around her waist. She thrust her hips forward, unable to control the maddening need for him.

He moved his hands to her butt and bent down and lifted her. She wrapped her legs around him, enjoying him hot and hard between her legs. She'd never wanted anything as much as she wanted him inside her. Her panties were wet with need, and her core throbbed painfully. He carried her to one of the folding tables, then set her on it. He hadn't broken the kiss, and she searched wildly for his hand, but he was ahead of her.

As she plundered his mouth, he put his hand on her knee and ran it up her thigh. She moaned, arching her hips instinctively to encourage him. Her hands were still around his neck, and she ran them down to his chest. He put his palm between her legs, pressing against the silk of her panties, and she moaned. The warmth of his hand provided temporary relief. She pulsed against his hand, then broke the kiss. "More, Dev, I need more."

He didn't hesitate. He slipped the fabric of her panties aside and put his thumb on her core. The rush of heat that flew through her belly was so intense that she sucked in her breath. His lips moved from her mouth to her neck as his thumb circled her clit. "More," she said hoarsely. She needed him inside her, filling her, pumping into her, releasing her.

He slipped a finger inside her but kept his thumb on her core. She gasped and grabbed a fistful of his shirt, unsure if she could keep her balance on the table. Her entire body throbbed with pleasure. "I need you," she begged, so close to the edge, she couldn't stand it. She thrust her chest forward. His mouth moved down her chest. He pushed down the v-neckline of her dress and she reached down and undid the knot holding the wraparound dress in place. The front of the dress opened and he pushed the lace bra aside. His mouth gripped her nipple just as he slid another finger inside her, and she lost her mind.

When the last waves of ecstasy finally subsided, she dropped her head on his chest, feeling satiated yet wanting more. He extracted his fingers from her, and a moaning sound of protest escaped her lips.

"I'm sorry I didn't wait for you," she said, somewhat embarrassed. She'd been so caught up in her own pleasure that she really hadn't considered his. She hadn't been prepared to orgasm so quickly. It almost never happened to her.

He kissed her ear, and another ripple of pleasure tore through her. She extended her arm and touched him through his pants. He was still hard, and she started to unbuckle his belt. Maybe her unlucky streak with men was over. If she could keep Dev hard this long, after she'd already orgasmed, maybe there was hope for them. Maybe she wasn't a cold fish after all.

Her hands trembled as she tugged on the belt. Dev put a hand on hers.

"Caitlyn, no."

She froze. He didn't want her. He'd pleased her because she'd asked—no, begged, no, *accosted*—him for it, but he didn't want her back.

She pulled away from him, adjusted her bra, pulled her underwear back in place, and re-tied her dress. Her breaths were coming faster than they should but she couldn't slow down the beating of her heart. It was happening again. Why had she forgotten that this was what happened every time? Why did she think things would work with Dev? *Because things have been different with him.*

"Hey, are you okay? Did we go too far?"

She couldn't meet his gaze. There was no way she was letting him see the tears brimming in her eyes.

She shook her head, unable to speak. She hopped off the table, nearly tripping as her feet landed unsteadily. He caught her and lifted her chin so she was forced to look at him.

"Hey, what did I do wrong?"

The traitorous tears wouldn't stay put, and his face crumpled. "Oh my God, did I hurt you? What did I do? Please say something."

Somehow, she was making things worse. *Why can't I get hold of myself?* The one thing she could always do was put on her armor and extract herself with dignity.

She took a breath. "If you didn't want to be with me, you just had to say so."

"What? You think I don't want you?" He pulled her into his embrace and held her tight, pressing his body against her. "Does it feel like I don't want you?"

It sure doesn't.

"Then what is it?"

He kissed her forehead tenderly, then trailed kisses down her cheek. Despite the doubt flooding her thoughts, her body responded immediately, wanting, needing him. She pressed against him, her body seeking reassurance that she did indeed turn him on.

"I don't want our first time to be in a barn. Call me a hopeless romantic, but I want it to be special." He kissed her neck. "I want to take my time, treat you the way you should be treated." He nibbled on her earlobe, his breath warm, and her entire body molded itself to him. She moaned sinfully. *I don't want to wait. I want you right now.* "I want to see you naked. I want your hands all over my body. I want us to have the whole night to enjoy each other, not just this stolen moment."

How could she argue with an offer like that?

"Tonight," he promised.

Eight

"No, Ma! I haven't seen her biodata, and I'm not interested," Dev said, his face reflecting the frustration he felt. His mother was on a video call with him, so he couldn't even fake that he was in the middle of a meeting. Ma had caught on to that trick and insisted on scheduled video calls.

"Dev, your younger siblings are married. I talked to *Pandit-ji* and he said the stars are aligned for you to marry."

"I'm only twenty-eight, Ma. It's the time to build my business, not get saddled with family obligations."

"Your father was married when he was twenty. Do you think he built his empire by himself? Why do you think a wife is a liability?"

Because I've seen how my siblings' spouses have drained them, financially and emotionally. He loved his brother and sister, but he'd witnessed them slowly giving up their goals in favor of what their spouses wanted. His brother hadn't wanted children, yet his wife convinced him to have two. She was pregnant with her second when the first was barely two. His sister, the cutthroat businesswoman, had agreed to quit her job and stay home to help her husband with his elder-care duties. He didn't want to be forced to make the same choices. He had a specific plan for his business. First the restaurant in Royal, then a chain across the United States. He needed to be a free agent, not saddled with a wife.

So what're you doing with Caitlyn? He pushed that thought aside. He'd been honest with Caitlyn from the beginning about how he planned to leave.

"It doesn't matter anyway. I'm dating someone." He knew it was a dangerous thing to admit to his mother, but it would temporarily get her off his back. At least buy him some time until he was back in New York and could avoid her in person.

"Very nice, very nice. Can I see her picture?"

He rolled his eyes. "How about asking me what type of person she is, Ma? Why is it straight to the looks for you."

"*Aaare*, you think I haven't learned your type by now? You want the impossible in a woman. She has to be intelligent, she has to be kind and caring, she has to be this, she has to be that. All the goddesses in the Vedas combined couldn't meet your requirements for a woman. If you selected a girl for your-self, then she must be something. So, I want to see her picture."

He knew why his mother wanted to see Caitlyn's picture. First to make sure she was real and he wasn't just making an excuse. Second, so she could see what attracted him. He knew it was a bad idea, but maybe complying would get his mother off the phone faster.

He'd already texted Caitlyn to see if she wanted to come with him to check out a restaurant location, and she'd just texted him back asking what time. He wanted it to be as soon as possible. He was eager to spend more time with her. But first things first.

He pulled up her picture on his laptop. She was on several local committees and boards, and many of them had a picture of her on their website. His fa-vorite was a standard yearbook-style picture where she had only the slightest smile on her face. It was meant to be serious, but he loved that photo. She looked so innocent and sexy, wearing a strand of pearls around her long, elegant neck, her makeup minimal and her wavy hair down around her shoul-ders. It had only been a few hours since he'd seen her, but he was already anxious to see her again. He had the whole night planned out.

She'd sparked an idea this morning, and he'd called Greg, who had found a promising place. Dev had already been to see it and was going to take Cait-lyn there in the evening. Then they'd pick up Italian from her favorite restaurant and bring it back to his hotel room, where he hoped to have her to himself all night and all day tomorrow.

He shared his screen with his mother, who gasped.

"*Wah!* You have good taste. She is beautiful."

He didn't know why, but his mother's approval sat well with him, even though he hated that fact. He was trying to become an independent man, but somewhere inside was still a child who sought his parent's approval.

"Is she Indian?"

He flinched. He'd hoped the conversation wouldn't come to that. He knew how his parents felt. They expected him to marry someone whose ethnic background was from India. Even though he and his siblings had been born and raised in the US and lived like Americans, his parents firmly believed that someone who wasn't Indian couldn't understand the closeness of their family and their values. Dev had disagreed even before he met Caitlyn but even more so after getting to know her. She knew exactly what it meant to put her family's needs before her own. She'd been doing it all her life. In many ways, she lived her family values far better than he did.

"No, she is not."

"She's definitely not white. Then what is she? Mexican?"

He winced. Typical of her generation, social standing and general lack of tact, his mother did not feel the need to filter her bluntness.

"No."

"Dev," his mother said warningly, and he knew her patience was wearing thin.

He sighed. "She's biracial, Mom, half white, half African American."

His mother was silent. When she finally spoke, it was worse than he'd braced himself for. "Are you trying to punish me?"

He stayed silent. It was a rhetorical question. He studied his mother's pinched face. She was only forty-eight, having married when she was eighteen and had him when she was twenty. Yet she looked like she was in her thirties, her face unmarred by wrinkles and perfectly made up with eyeliner and dark red lipstick. She wore diamond solitaires in her ears, and her hair was dyed perfectly in shades of black and reddish brown where the gray would have been. Dev got his green eyes from her, but when they stared at him from his mother's face, he felt a chill down his spine.

"Do you know what it will do to our social standing if you marry a Black woman?"

He didn't bother correcting her as to Caitlyn's race. In truth, he didn't know how she identified. For all he knew, his mother might be right. He'd only just realized that he hadn't bothered to ask.

"You are the most eligible bachelor in our community. You can have any desi girl you want from around the globe. I get no less than three offers a day for you. For good girls, educated girls, beautiful girls. Girls who know our language, our culture, and can teach it to your children. I've given you a lot of slack thinking you just need some time to go do some *maasti*, and if that's what this is, I'm fine with it. But I will tell you in no uncertain terms that you will not marry a girl who is not Indian."

"Ma!" he said, exasperated. "Who is talking marriage? I'm just dating her." It was the coward's way out of the conversation, but he was in no mood to have it right now. He knew how his parents felt, and there was no point in battling with them unless there was a reason to do so. He was nowhere close to marrying anyone, and Caitlyn was far from a contender. It was clear from their conversations that she was tied to Royal. She had no interest in traveling or leaving her comfort zone.

Appeased, his mother gave him a small smile. "Have whatever fun you want. You know I'm very modern thinking that way. As long as you know what we expect of you."

How could I not?

He managed to get his mother off his back by scheduling their next video chat and with a promise that he would read the biodata she'd sent of the latest wife prospective. The biodata was a résumé-like dating profile with a picture, their likes, dislikes, education, etc. He'd wait a day to pretend as if he'd studied it, then send an email to his mother saying he didn't like it. Since the next video call was a few days from now, that would give her enough time to calm down.

His phone pinged, reminding him that Caitlyn was

waiting for an answer from him. He quickly made plans to see her in a few hours.

"Who are you texting with?" Alice asked suspiciously.

Caitlyn guiltily clicked a button on her phone to darken the screen as Alice leaned over. They were in Caitlyn's bedroom, which remained largely unchanged from when her mother had redecorated it during her teenage years. A queen bed with a gray upholstered headboard stood in the middle, decorated with an elegant silver-and-gray comforter and pillow set. A small couch stood underneath a bay window with end tables on either side and two chairs across for a cozy sitting room. But the two women were sitting cross-legged on the bed like they had when they were in college. Alice and Caitlyn hadn't gone to the same high school, as Caitlyn had been in private school and Alice had gone to the public school. Yet they'd met in college and instantly bonded over their Royal roots. More than once, Caitlyn wished she'd become friends with Alice instead of Jax.

"How many have we gotten done?" Caitlyn asked, changing the subject.

Alice rolled her eyes. "What does it matter, we have like a million more to do. I can't believe I let you talk me into this."

"It's for a good cause." They were making brown bags for the foster kids. The snacks fed the kids on the weekends when there was no school breakfast or lunch. Normally, the high school kids packed the bags, but it was prom weekend, so they'd been short on volunteers and Caitlyn had agreed to pick up the slack. One of the Lattimore charities she oversaw funded the snack bags. She knew Alice wasn't really complaining—she had offered to help.

"I still think you need to give Russ a chance."

"Alice, he's not interested in me."

"Listen, I know Dev. Russ always brought him home for Thanksgiving because his own family didn't celebrate the holiday. He's a nice guy, he really is, but he's never going to be serious about anyone until his business is established. He's pretty much said so to me and Russ."

"Who said we're getting serious? I just asked him to help me practice my conversational skills and get comfortable around men. Didn't you tell me that's what I need to do?"

"Hardly! I told you to date a nice guy. Like Russ."

"The guy who personifies the love-'em-and-leave-'em motto?" Caitlyn said with a tinge of annoyance in her voice. Alice sometimes forgot how much time she spent lamenting Russ's dating exploits.

"He's changed, and he's ready to settle down."

"No, *you're* ready for him to change and settle down. There's a difference."

Alice glared at her, and Caitlyn softened her tone, well aware that she'd be just as defensive if someone tried to tell her that she was wrong about her brothers. "Listen, Russ is a great guy, no doubt. But it's a little hard to think of him as anyone other than your brother.

There's no spark, you understand?" Alice didn't look convinced.

"I don't want this to affect our friendship, Alice. How would you feel if I tried to set you up with one of my brothers and you didn't like him? Could you please let this go?"

Alice sighed. "Okay, I'll lay off Russ. Will you tell me whether the mystery man you're texting is Dev?"

Caitlyn sighed. "Yes."

"I knew it!" Alice screamed.

"A mystery man, huh."

Caitlyn groaned as she turned to see Alexa in the doorway. Her long black curls were loose, and she was wearing a gray T-shirt and bike shorts, her standard gym uniform. The last thing Caitlyn needed was for Alexa to get involved with the conversation regarding Dev. It was so rare for Alexa to be home, she didn't want their time together to be about her dating life.

Alexa homed in on Alice, knowing she was the weaker link. "Nice to see you, Alice." She sat on the bed and picked up one of the bags to fill, so Caitlyn could hardly object. "So, you have a mystery man. Looks like a picked a good weekend to make a trip home. Spill."

Alexa had always intimidated Alice a little. It was the lawyer in her—she had a way looking at you like she could read your mind. Alice shifted on the bed. "That's what I've been trying to get out of Caitlyn, but it's a secret mystery man. Maybe you can get more out of her."

Devious. Caitlyn glared at her best friend as Alexa turned to her. Caitlyn knew it was fruitless—Alexa would hound her until she gave in. "As Alice well knows, the not-so-secret and utterly unmysterious man is Dev Mallik, Russ's best friend. I met him at dinner at Alice's house."

"So dish some more. What's he like?" Alexa pressed.

"He's nice. He's in Royal to open a restaurant, and I agreed to show him around town. We've gone out to dinner five or six times and talked on the phone a few times. No biggie."

Alexa and Alice exchanged glances, which irritated Caitlyn. They were both supposed to be on her side. "What is it?" Caitlyn asked.

"You met him two weeks ago and you've already been out with him five or six times," Alexa didn't bother to hide the surprise in her voice.

She had actually seen Dev more than that, but Caitlyn wasn't going to add fuel to the fire. Each date had been more frustratingly platonic than the last. Dev had stayed true to his word. While there was the inadvertent hand or shoulder brush, until this morning there hadn't been anything sexual. They'd sampled all the Royal restaurants like a pair of food critics and decided that Dev had his work cut out for him. If he wanted to compete in the Royal restaurant business, he'd have to offer something extraordinary. Dev had talked about the chef he'd lined up for his restaurant and the dishes they were working on together, and Caitlyn was impressed and genuinely looking forward to the new place in Royal. The only hiccup had been that Dev hadn't liked the places Russ had lined up for him as potential locations, and he'd gone through Greg's list too.

Then this morning happened. She didn't know whether it was the knowledge that he might leave earlier than he was planning, or the sexual tension that had been simmering between them, but she'd been ready to take things to the next level with him. She needed to see whether her practice relationship could turn into a real one. Tonight would be the test.

"Earth to Caitlyn." Alexa snapped her fingers.

Caitlyn turned back to the conversation. "So what if I've been out with him a few times? I'm helping him get to know Royal, and he's helping me with my conversational skills. It's not like we're headed down the aisle. It's a temporary friendship."

"For you, darlin', that many dates is a serious relationship," Alice chimed in.

Caitlyn shot Alice and Alexa an irritated look.

"I'm just worried that you're getting involved with someone who's going to be leaving town in a couple of weeks," Alice said.

I'm worried about the same thing. "He's planning to stay a little longer." She didn't know if that was true, but she hoped she could convince him to stay longer if things went well tonight.

"For how long? Once he finds a location, he's going to leave and go back to New York," Alice said.

"And he'll be back occasionally to check on his

restaurant," Caitlyn said, hating how defensive she sounded. "We can see each other then."

"I thought you said this was temporary," Alexa said softly, and Caitlyn cursed under her breath. Trust the lawyer to find the flaw in her argument.

She knew it was the norm in her family to baby Caitlyn, but she was a grown woman now. She knew how to handle her affairs. *Just like you handled Jax,* a condescending inner voice jibed at her.

"Look, I know you guys mean well, but trust me to make my choices. I know full well Dev is not from around here, and that he's going to leave. I know whatever I have with him is short term. I don't need you guys to explain it to me like I'm a teenager with a crush."

Alice cleared her throat. "There's something else you should know about Dev."

She shifted on the bed, and Caitlyn lost her cool. "Out with it, Alice."

Both Alice and Alexa raised their brows but wisely didn't comment on Caitlyn's tone.

"Russ wanted to set me up with Dev, because he's a nice guy and Russ knows I want to settle down and get on the marriage train. Dev confided in him that he can't marry someone who isn't Indian. Apparently, his family is quite traditional."

Her heart fisted. She and Dev had never talked about marriage, but somewhere in the back of her mind, she realized they'd actively avoided the topic. He talked about his family and all the expectations they weighed down on him but never what it meant for his romantic future, just his professional one.

"Wow, let's just hit pause here a second, guys. Everyone's been harassing me to get out more. I go out on a few dates and here you are evaluating whether he's marriage material and questioning whether we have a future together. Haven't we fast-forwarded a bit too much?"

Both Alice and Alexa had the grace to look sheepish. "Sorry, darlin', I just don't want to see you hurt, and aside from Jax, I've never seen you spend so much time with one guy," Alice said. "Russ said all Dev can talk about is you. I'm seeing things moving too fast and just want to make sure you don't get hurt."

Alexa nodded. "I'm glad you're out and dating. It's time you moved on from Jax."

"How many times do I need to tell you that I'm over Jax?" Caitlyn tried to keep her voice level. She knew she'd fallen apart after Jax, but could anyone really blame her, given their history?

Alexa leaned forward and took Caitlyn's hand in hers. "When you were six years old, you loved this old horse called Shooting Star."

Caitlyn nodded. She remembered that horse clearly—he was an Appaloosa, a beautiful white horse with brown dots and a sandy blond mane.

"You loved that horse so much you rode him every day, rain or shine. But he ended up with colic that wasn't treatable, and the vet recommended we put him down. You were devastated. No matter how hard we tried, you refused to believe that Shooting Star couldn't be cured."

"I was ten," Caitlyn said defensively. "And as I remember, he was eventually put down."

Alexa squeezed her hand. "Do you remember that you spent two days and two nights sitting by his stall, refusing to let the vet take him? You were adamant that he would heal on his own, that your sheer force of will could cure him. Daddy didn't want to forcibly remove you, so we took turns staying with you until you fell asleep out of sheer exhaustion. That's when we were finally able to take Shooting Star."

"I don't know what all this has to do with Dev." Caitlyn shifted on the bed. She wanted this conversation to be over with.

"It has to do with you, Caitlyn," Alexa said gently. "You have so much love in your heart, and you give it all to the people you care about. Sometimes you give too much. Even though I wasn't here, I could tell that things were moving too fast with Jax, but I didn't say anything, and I wish I had."

Caitlyn softened her voice and looked directly at Alexa. "I'm not a fragile baby. I know I'm loved and that I have an amazing support system…" she blew a kiss to Alice and squeezed Alexa's hand "…but you guys need to trust that I can take care of myself. I'm doing exactly what I set out to—I'm going out with someone where I know there's no chance of a future, so I can relax and get some flirting practice." She injected just the right amount of casualness in her voice, but her stomach churned painfully.

Had she really thought through where things were going with Dev? She'd been so focused on how easy it was with him, convinced that it would end at any second, that she hadn't really considered the opposite possibility—*what if it went well?*

Nine

"Little thing like you should not be carryin' those big boxes," Ol'Fred bellowed. Caitlyn set down the boxes containing the snack bags they'd packed.

Ol'Fred stood where he always did, behind a wood checkout counter. His place looked more like a gas station pit stop than the fancy places that surrounded him, but Ol'Fred's shop had been here since the day Royal was founded, and no one told Ol'Fred how to run his general store. He carried basic groceries, knickknacks, tools—anything that someone doing real work in Royal might need on an urgent basis. He also carried specialty drinks, high-end whiskeys and wines that forced the elite of Royal to trudge to his store. It was the only place in town where every resident of Royal could shop.

"I'm not as fragile as I look. Can I leave these here? Yolanda said she'd pick them up in the morning."

"You don't have to ask. Y'know I'd do anything for the kids." He called out to one of his store hands to take the boxes.

Ol'Fred pulled out a can of Fanta and handed it to her. Caitlyn smiled and popped the tab, careful not let the fizz spill over. It was their tradition since she was a little girl. Her mother never let her have the orange drink because it was full of sugar, so Ol'Fred would sneak it to her.

"You just missed Jax."

Caitlyn looked around the store. "Don't worry, he's gone." She didn't know whether she was relieved or disappointed. They'd done the avoidance dance for a year—she needed to get it over with.

"You never did tell me what happened with you and Jax." Ol'Fred's tone was fatherly.

Caitlyn leaned over and kissed Ol'Fred on the cheek. "What do you always say, one day a rooster, the next day a feather duster? That was mine and Jax's relationship."

"Guess I'm gonna have to leave it with you."

She thanked him for the Fanta and walked out of the store. Just as she opened the door, she bumped into someone, dropping the almost-full can of Fanta. She murmured an apology and bent down to pick up the can before it made more of a mess.

"I see Ol'Fred is still taking care of you."

She froze. A knot formed and twisted in her stomach. She took a breath then stood. "Jax."

He smiled at her, but she couldn't bring herself to do the same. He was wearing his standard-issue basketball shorts and a T-shirt. His hair was freshly close-cropped.

They stood for a moment, staring, each unsure what to say to the other. Jax spoke first. "Listen, I think we should talk. We've avoided each other long enough. We can't leave things like this."

She nodded. Wordlessly, they walked to the park, to their bench. It was the place where they used to meet to do their homework; it was the place where he'd told her that her father had paid for his tuition to her exclusive private school so she'd have a friend; it was the place where they'd met when he first came back from college; it was the place where they'd first kissed. It was only fitting that it be the bench where they finally closed their relationship.

Her throat was tight. She didn't know how to begin, what to say. He didn't seem to have that problem.

"Look, Caitlyn, I'm sorry about the last time we were together. I shouldn't have left like that, and I shouldn't have said the things I did. I hope you didn't dwell on it."

She'd played that night in her mind for months after their breakup.

"Did you mean it? What you said?" She hated the high-pitched tone of her voice, but she needed to know whether they were words of anger or whether he'd truly meant them.

He was silent. "We've been friends for a long time, Jax. I need you to be honest with me."

He sighed. "Look, your father might have paid for my tuition and asked me to be your friend, but he didn't make you my best friend. You did. You were the only one who was nice to me at that high-brow place. I felt intimidated by that crowd, being one of the few Black kids, being the only kid who didn't summer in Europe and on and on. But you gave me confidence—you treated me like I belonged there. That's why we became best friends. It had nothing to do with your father paying my way"

She gave him a small smile. "You were the only kid in school I liked. It was easy to be your friend."

"The only reason I told you about your father paying my tuition is because I didn't want you to find out from someone other than me. What I didn't tell you is that you weren't just my best friend. You were also my childhood crush. But my ma worked for your family. If things didn't go well between us, it would've meant ruin for my family. I had no choice. I could only be your best friend."

"That's what brought us back together when you returned home after college"

"But that's just it. Four years had passed. I was a different person than I was in high school. And I hoped you had changed, too."

"What exactly does that mean?"

"Remember Declan Grayson?"

Her cheeks warmed. "That was high school, Jax."

"It was junior year. You were so in love with him. You did anything he asked of you but then, just like that, you dumped him. I tried talking to you about it, but you wouldn't tell me a thing."

"It that what this is about? Some old high school secret…"

He shook his head, but before he could say anything, she jumped in. "You want to know what happened with Declan? He was a high school crush. I went out with him, and he wanted to go further physically than I cared to. I told him I wanted to wait and he didn't, so I dumped him. Pardon me if I didn't feel comfortable talking to my male best friend about how I hated some other guy's groping."

The knot in her stomach twisted painfully. Perhaps this had all been a bad idea. What had she hoped to gain from this conversation? She knew what the issue was, had experienced it ever since high school.

"I knew all about it, Caitlyn. Declan told the whole school you were a prude and some other not-so-nice words. That's not why I bring him up." He sighed. "You put your heart and soul into everything you do. Including relationships. You went all in for Declan. You hardly knew him, and yet you were making little hearts in your notebook and writing *Mrs. Caitlyn Grayson*."

Heat rose up her neck and to her cheeks. She should have known Jax would've noticed her school-girl notes. "I was sixteen, Jax. Give me a break."

She wished she had the Fanta can that she'd just thrown away to clear the nasty taste in her mouth.

Jax rubbed his neck, a gesture she knew well. "What are you trying to say, Jax? Just spit it out."

"When I came back to town, I wanted to give us a chance. I didn't want to go through life wondering what might have been with you. But you wanted to pick up as if no time had passed. It was like we went from catching up over coffee to being engaged in one day. You didn't even bother to get to know me."

"I do know you, Jax. We spent four years together."

"When we were kids."

He gave her a small smile. "I'm not that person anymore. Do you know, for example, that I led a Black Lives Matter protest in DC? Or that I took the LSATs to see if I can get into law school to become a civil rights lawyer?"

That stung. Caitlyn narrowed her eyes. "You'd only just gotten into town—we hardly had time to talk."

"That's my point exactly. You didn't bother to get to know me fully before jumping into our relationship. We'd barely begun, and you were already showing me off at every Cattleman's Club event, dragging me here and there every single weekend. You were even making wedding plans."

Caitlyn shook her head. "That's not true, Jax. I was enthusiastic about our relationship because of our past. Just like you, I'd thought about us on and off through high school, but I didn't want to ruin our friendship. We weren't strangers."

"But we were, Caitlyn. We were old friends who should have taken the time to get to know each other, but we jumped right into a serious relationship without going through the dating part first. I'm not saying it was all you. I did it, too. I came back and found you grown into a beautiful woman and couldn't help falling into the fantasy you painted for us. After six months it just all came crashing down, the reality of what we'd been doing."

"So it's my fault. I put too much pressure on our relationship."

"That's not what I'm saying. I think it was both our faults. We let things move too quickly."

She shook her head and stood. "Are you done with what you had to say?"

He hung his head, then nodded slowly. "I'm not handling this right, but I want you to know that I care about you very much."

Just not enough. That's the part he didn't want to say, but she understood. She wanted to tell him that she'd trusted him, as a former friend, as her boyfriend, and that he'd broken her heart. But she couldn't bring herself to do that. The all-too-familiar knot in her stomach had grown and risen up to her throat, choking her. At least he didn't refer to her as a cold fish again.

"Thanks for the talk. Have a nice life," she managed to cough out, then walked away as quickly as she could without breaking into a run.

One thing was for certain—she wouldn't make the same mistakes with Dev. She wasn't getting into anything serious with him.

Ten

It was the first time he'd picked Caitlyn up from the Lattimore ranch, and Dev couldn't help be impressed. The ranch seemed to be an endless sprawl of perfectly landscaped lawn and picturesque barns. No peeling paint and rusted doors here. The one-mile drive from the front gate to the mansion was lined with perfectly trimmed hedges. Russ hadn't been kidding when he'd pitched the idea of Dev opening a restaurant in Royal—the kind of wealth here put the fancy Manhattan penthouse circle to shame.

The property he'd seen today had the potential to make not only his dreams come true, but also Caitlyn's. He couldn't wait to show it to her. He'd already spoken to the chef and restaurant manager he'd lined up and walked them through the space on video.

They agreed with his plans. All he needed was for Caitlyn to get on board.

They'd only known each other a short time, but he'd connected with her on an intellectual and emotional level. She understood the two parts of him, the one that belonged to his family and the one that longed to be an independent man. Getting into business was the perfect way to keep her in his life. It would give him time to sort out their romantic relationship.

She was waiting for him under the portico of a circular driveway. She looked stunning in a strappy ice-blue dress with a crisscross design that gave him a peekaboo view of her lovely back. The dress ended midthigh, showing off her shapely legs. It was the kind of sexy dress he'd never seen her in before. Her hair was left loose around her face, not straight and pressed as it normally was, but curly and wild, just the way he liked it. She was wearing flat shoes, and he was glad she had thought practically.

Before the car fully stopped, she tapped on the window. He unlocked the car, intending to get out and open the passenger side for her, but she yanked open the door, got in and smiled. "Let's go."

"In a hurry to get out?"

"Yes!" she breathed. "If my siblings find out you're picking me up, trust me, they'll be all over us and will monopolize the entire evening. You can forget any plans you may have."

Is that the only reason you don't want me meeting your family?

He punched the accelerator, eager to get to their destination. "Listen, your idea this morning gave me one of my own. So, I asked Greg to look, and he found the perfect place."

"That's great."

"But I need you to say yes to make the place work."

"Why me?" He caught the tentative fear in her voice but pushed it aside. He was being mysterious, after all.

He reached over and patted her hand. "You'll see."

Greg had given him the keys to the small ranch. Dev wanted privacy to explain his idea to Caitlyn. He had no idea how she'd react. He hadn't let himself fully consider what he would do if she said no. Because in that case, he was out of options in Royal and would have to move on. Already he'd spent more time here than he should have. Although he'd given himself a month, he'd seen most of the properties that would have been suitable for his restaurant in the first few days, but he'd kept looking. Not because he didn't have other places to go, but because he wanted to see where things went with Caitlyn.

He'd come to that realization after talking with his mother. He rarely shared information about who he was dating, and he knew his mother would have an issue with Caitlyn not being Indian, but he'd told her anyway. He'd told her so that his mother could start getting used to the idea of Caitlyn. He'd told her because he'd never met a woman he felt as comfortable with as Caitlyn. The fact that he hadn't even slept with her and was thinking these thoughts made it all the harder to ignore his feelings for her. She understood him, really listened to what he wanted without trying to impose what she wanted. Tonight was the ultimate test to see if she felt as strongly for him as he did for her. Would she go along with his plans? Would she be willing to share and mold her dream with his?

"We're going to the east side of Royal?"

He nodded. "Yes, we've exhausted everything on the west side, so I asked Greg to expand the search to all of Royal. Why? Is that a problem?"

She stayed quiet for a few minutes, as if formulating her thoughts. He snuck a look at her and saw frown lines on her forehead. "East Royal doesn't have the social demographics you're looking for to support the luxury restaurant you're envisioning."

He smiled. "You mean it's the poor part of town."

"Yes," she said quietly. "And I don't mean it disparagingly, I just mean that's where the working-class families live. They can't pay the type of prices you're considering. The wealthy ranchers on the west side aren't really going to drive to a high-end restaurant on this side of town."

"I have an idea for that," he said.

"Now I'm really intrigued. You know, Ol'Fred's shop is the only one on Main Street that's for regular people and not there to cater to the hoity-toity of Royal. It would be nice to have another place like that in Royal."

"Aren't you one of those hoity-toitys?" he asked playfully.

She nodded. "I absolutely am. Which is why I really want to do that horse camp. I know my family participates in boards and charities, but that stuff barely scratches the surface. Half the time I'm not even sure where all the money goes. I want to do something where I can see the results in front of me, not on a piece of paper."

He smiled. "Any news on the oil rights claim on your ranch?"

She shook her head. "We're still waiting for the private eye to find whether the deed Heath Thurston has is valid. We looked through our own family papers but haven't found anything."

She sighed. "I just want this to be over with so I can start working on my camp. I thought by now we'd have some resolution."

"Maybe it's for the best?"

"What do you mean?"

"I could fund my restaurant from my trust fund. Or by simply selling one of the cars my father has gifted me that mostly sits in a New York garage at a rent that constitutes most people's annual salary. But I didn't touch any of that money. Do you know why?"

"Because you want to be your own man."

"That's part of it, but it's a lot more than that. Everything in my family is intertwined—our home, our finances, our social lives, you name it, and it's all one big happy family. The problem with that is there's no room for real disagreements. If I want to go against my family, I can't. This is my way of ensuring I have an escape chute if I need it."

He pulled into the driveway of the small ranch Greg had found for him. He parked the car and looked at Caitlyn.

"You really think you're going to need an escape from your family?"

"I'd rather not find out."

She shifted in her seat. "I can't imagine a scenario where I'd need to flee from my family."

"There are a lot of expectations in my family that may not exist in yours."

"Like who you marry?"

His heart slammed into his chest. He didn't want to talk about this now. He wanted this evening to be about them and their relationship. He needed to know whether she felt the same connection he did. Whether her heart was going in the same direction as his. It was too soon to contemplate the future with a woman he'd only known for two weeks. He knew that intellectually, but his gut and his heart said something different. What he and Caitlyn had was special. Unique. Wasn't it? Sitting here with her, it certainly felt that way, but the conversation with his mother had unsettled him. He'd found himself anxious to make sure that Caitlyn shared his feelings about their relationship, that she was also seeing a future for them.

She was waiting for a response.

"I will marry whom I want," he said firmly.

"Your parents don't get a say?"

"Does your family get a say in who you marry?"

She paused then shook her head. "They'd never stand in the way of my happiness. They do have strong opinions about who I date, and I'm sure any man I bring home will have to stand up to a CIA-level interrogation, but ultimately they'll support my decision."

He wished he could say the same thing about his family.

"Let's go see this place."

It was nice sized property, nestled on a relatively flat area of land bordered by trees. They drove up to the ranch house, which was a charming, sprawling one-level.

"I don't know this property. Who lived here?"

"From what Greg told me, it belonged to a Mr. and Mrs. Fredrick. They left the property to their son, and he's recently decided to sell."

He opened the front door and they stepped into a large foyer with hardwood floors.

"You want to convert the house into a restaurant?"

He nodded and pointed out the various rooms. "It's already got a large kitchen. I'd only have to put in commercial appliances. The rest of the house can be easily converted into a dining room. The smaller rooms can be for small private groups."

She peeked into the formal dining room. It was a cozy space with a rectangular dining table that sat ten people. "I can see my family eating in this room. And the house has so many windows, it feels bigger than it is."

He nodded.

"I like the feel of this place. I can totally see seating on the porch and the back deck, and a beautiful dining room on this main level with the current bedrooms as private meeting areas for business dinners. But the Royal elite still aren't going to drive all the way over here."

"I have a plan for that," he said. But the plan hinged on her. His stomach flipped. The next few minutes would tell him how she felt about him. In a way, the next moments would decide whether or not he stayed in Royal.

"Looks like the old owners took really good care of the house. The floors are polished, the baseboards are clean…and they're mostly moved out. Why hasn't it sold yet? The real estate market in Royal is pretty strong."

"Well, there's a rather big catch that's in the property covenant."

She raised a brow, and he led her to the back door and opened it. She gasped. The twenty-acre backyard held two riding rings and two large barns. There were a couple of horses turned out into the rings, a black horse and a white one with black spots.

Caitlyn gasped. "I was not expecting this. Those horses are beautiful." She pointed to the black one. "That's actually a mustang—a pretty well-bred one, from what I can tell. And the other is an appaloosa." Her voice caught.

He placed a hand on the small of her back. She stiffened slightly. "What's wrong, Caitlyn?"

She shook her head. "Nothing. I used to have an appaloosa when I was a little girl. He died."

He placed an arm around her shoulders. "I'm sorry."

"It just brings up a painful memory."

He took a breath, wondering if now was the time to bring up his plans. *What the hell!* "Well, maybe it's a sign."

"Of what?"

"That this horse is meant to be yours."

She looked up at him, frowning. "I don't understand."

"The catch with this place is that it comes with those two stables that can take a total of twenty-some horses and those two beauties there. The owners want someone who will agree to take the horses and keep them together. Apparently they're bonded—whatever that means."

"It means they're attached to each other. Horses that bond together are hard to separate. They get sick if you do."

She was staring at the horses. "Let's go see them."

He pointed to the stairs leading down from the deck. As they approached the ring where the horses were roaming around, the appaloosa stopped and considered them. When they were within a few feet of the ring, the black mustang snorted, whinnied and reared.

Dev put a hand on her shoulder to hold her back. "Careful, Caitlyn, I don't know anything about these horses."

She smiled back at him, and his knees went weak. The setting sun backlit her in soft orange and yellow hues. *How can one woman be so stunningly, perfectly beautiful?* Despite his busy afternoon, there wasn't a moment that had gone by without him thinking about their morning together. Had that just been this morning? It seemed like a lifetime ago that she'd pulsed against his fingers and thrown her head back in such abandon that he'd nearly lost it. He'd been with enough women to know how to control himself. That he'd almost lost it with her told him there was something special about Caitlyn. Something so special that, for the first time in his life, he was intimidated by the thought of a night with her. What if he couldn't control himself? What if he couldn't live up to her expectations? What if he couldn't give her what she deserved?

He pushed the last thought out of his head. He didn't even know if she felt the same way about him. Before he started making plans, he needed to know that they were on the same page.

"Trust me," she said. "Stay back a little."

There was no way he was going to let her walk so dangerously close to the horses. He walked right behind her, ready to leap if the horses decided to jump the fence.

She began talking softly to the horses. "Good boy. That's right, you're a good boy." The appaloosa snorted and scuffed the earth with his hind leg. The mustang hung back.

Caitlyn bent down and tore some of the grass from

the earth. He did the same. "Not the grass—get the clover that's growing." She un-fisted her hand and showed him the green plant. She approached the horse slowly. When she got to the fence, she extended her arm. The appaloosa sniffed, then clopped over to her. He buried his nose in her hand, then ate the offered clover.

She petted his head and then rubbed behind his ear. The mustang whinnied, then joined his friend. Dev offered the clover he had picked to Caitlyn, and she fed the mustang. *Maybe this will go better than I thought.*

"Who is taking care of these horses if the owners moved out?"

He smiled. Trust her to be worried about the animals. "Greg said there's a ranch hand that comes by to feed, water and turn them out."

She rubbed the mustang's back. The horse was practically rubbing up against the fence begging for Caitlyn's touch. Dev knew the feeling.

"Well, he's not doing a great job. The horses need grooming. Looks like they haven't been brushed in ages. I'll call Greg and ask to talk with the ranch hand."

"You can do one better."

She turned to look at him, and the appaloosa buried his nose in her neck. She automatically smiled and started rubbing the side of his face. Insanely, he felt jealous of the horse.

He cleared his throat. "Here's my idea. What if this was your horse camp?"

Her eyes widened. "What?"

"What if my restaurant wasn't just a restaurant but a riding club? We board horses for the rich and famous, and when they aren't riding those horses, you run your camp. This property is cheap enough that instead of renting like I had planned, I can buy it. This place can be ours. We can run it together. You run the stables, and I'll run the restaurant. I'm thinking I'll even create a café portion where I can serve up more family-priced dishes. Upscale restaurants in New York do that all the time—they have food trucks with better-priced dishes." He stopped. He'd been so busy pitching his idea that he hadn't stopped to look at her face.

She stepped away from the horses, and they began galloping around the ring.

"Caitlyn?"

She was turned away from him, so he placed a hand on her shoulder. "What is it?"

"Don't you think we're moving a bit fast?" Her voice was small.

"It's a business partnership," he said carefully. "Your idea this morning really resonated with me. I want to put my restaurant in this part of town. I want to create a place where everyone is welcome and can afford to eat. If we board some expensive horses, it'll attract the rich, and there's plenty of space here for you to run your camp without worrying about the claim on the Lattimore land."

"What exactly do you mean by a business relationship?"

Why was her voice so cagey? *Did I move too soon? Am I reading our relationship all wrong?*

"It's whatever you're comfortable with, Caitlyn. We can co-own the land. I can run the restaurant and you run the stables. This is just an idea, one I hoped we could work on together."

"What happens when our personal relationship ends?"

She said when, *not* if. He moved around so he was facing her. The sun had set quickly, and it was getting dark pretty fast. She refused to meet his eyes, and her body was so straight and stiff, it was as if one touch would send her fleeing. He put his hands behind him so he wouldn't be tempted to touch her. He could sense her fear. He'd felt it himself after realizing why he'd shown his mother her picture. He was falling in love with Caitlyn. For the first time in his life, he was thinking about a future that included more than just his business and family.

"You tell me. How far do you think our personal relationship can go?"

She still wouldn't look at him, intently studying the horses. "We hardly know each other, Dev."

He moved so he was in her line of sight. "Ask me anything you want to know. Go on—what is it that you want to know about me?"

"Is your family expecting you to marry someone Indian?"

He sucked in a breath then nodded. "Yes, but what they're expecting and what they'll get are two different things. I told you, I know I'll have disagreements with my family. They want me to marry someone they approve of, and the whole reason I want to be financially independent is that I don't want to be hostage to their standards. I want to marry the person I love."

"And how does this hypothetical love of yours fit into your plans to jet around the country building your empire?"

Her words were a knife in his gut. This was not at all how he'd hoped the conversation would go, but now that it had started, he had to finish it.

"Caitlyn, let's not talk in circles." He placed his hands gently on her shoulders, the lightest of touches. She stiffened but didn't move away from him. "Please look at me." She lifted her face, and his heart clenched painfully. Her brown eyes were shining, her nose and face flushed.

Had his words caused her grief? What had he done that was so wrong? Or was she misinterpreting what he was saying?

"I don't want there to be any confusion between us. What I'm saying is that I love you. I want to be with you. All this—" He gestured around them. "—is me trying to commit to you. I don't have everything worked out, but I don't want to. All I want to know is that you feel the same way about me and we'll figure out the rest together."

"Don't you think this relationship is moving a little fast? We've only known each other for two weeks and you're suggesting…"

Could she twist the knife any deeper into him?

She hadn't said she loved him back. Hadn't even acknowledged that he was making a grand gesture.

"What? What am I suggesting that's so scary to you?" He hated the annoyance in his voice, but he was fast losing control over his emotions. She didn't love him back. She didn't even see a future with him.

"We've only known each other two weeks. I told you the reason I haven't started the camp at my family ranch is because I don't want to start something and then have it yanked away from these children. They have nothing permanent in their lives. You blew into town with the intention of starting something here and leaving. How do I know that doesn't include me, too?"

"Because I'm telling you right now."

She stepped close to him, her mouth set in a firm line. "Can you tell me you'll stay in Royal if I ask you to?"

"That's not really fair."

"Why not?"

"You're not even ready to commit to a business proposition, but you want me to change my entire life plan and move here?"

"That's the point, Dev. Your plan is to open a restaurant and leave, but my life is here in Royal."

"So you expect me to upend my entire life, let go of all of my plans and move here to Royal?" He immediately regretted the hostility in his voice. He hadn't meant for the conversation to go this way. Perhaps he had jumped the gun.

She sighed, and a tear streamed down her cheek. He brushed it away with his finger. She grabbed his hand and kissed it. "I can't do this, Dev. I'm sorry, I can't."

Eleven

"I don't understand, Caitlyn." Alice was sitting on the pool lounger staring at her. This time Caitlyn was the one who'd drunk most of the chardonnay that sat between them. It had been two days since she'd seen Dev. After she'd refused to talk anymore, he had dropped her at her house and left. Since then, he hadn't texted or called. He hadn't responded to the text she'd sent that night saying she was sorry.

Alice had come over unannounced when she'd heard the story from Russ. "You know he's planning to leave tomorrow."

Her heart lurched. The last couple of days had been a jumble of emotions for her. The conversations with Alexa and Alice, with Jax, and then with Dev had all crashed into one tightly knotted tangle that she couldn't separate no matter how hard she tried.

"Look, I know I was against you and Dev getting together, but I can't see you like this. Russ says Dev is a mess. He's never seen the poor guy like that." She moved from her pool lounger to Caitlyn's. It was a rare cloudy and cool day so they were both in their sundresses enjoying the weather. Alice put an arm around Caitlyn. "What happened, darlin'? Did things not go well in bed?"

Trust Alice not to mince words. "Not this time. We didn't even try." Though that was not completely true. That morning in the barn was imprinted on her. She hadn't forgotten how her body had responded to him.

Alice waited patiently. Caitlyn's throat was tight. "It's Jax. I saw him, and we talked."

Alice hugged her tighter. "Oh, darlin', why didn't you call me? What did that rascal say to you?"

"Nothing that wasn't true. He pointed out that I jumped right into the relationship without even getting to know the man he'd become. That I put so much pressure on the relationship that it was inevitable for it to fail." She filled Alice in on their entire conversation. "He didn't say anything about our last night together, but he didn't need to. He blames the pressure I put on him—that was clear."

Alice gasped. "That little turd. How dare he?" She turned toward Caitlyn and squeezed her shoulders. "You listen to me. When he came back to town, you're the first person he asked about. He was just as hot 'n' heavy into it as you were."

Caitlyn hiccupped as the tears rolled down her cheek. "He's right, though. As soon as he came back to town and we started dating, I was hearing wedding bells. I put my entire life on hold for Jax. And I'm doing the same thing with Dev, putting my plans for the camp on the back burner."

"That's not what you're doing. You put your plans on hold because of that claim on the Lattimore land, not because of Dev."

Caitlyn shook her head. "When Dev took me to that ranch, I realized that I should have been the one to have found it. He's right, it is the perfect place for my camp, but I was so focused on Dev that I didn't know the ideal ranch went up for sale. I missed it completely."

"Caitlyn." She picked up the bottle of wine and topped up both their drinks. Caitlyn gulped a big sip of her wine. She knew that determined look on Alice's face—she was about to get a lecture.

"You are the most loving person I know. You dedicate yourself to the people and the projects in your life. That's why you stuff snack packs in your free time and run yourself ragged doing all the Lattimore business your siblings don't want to take on. That's who you are. Jax wasn't just some guy you dated. You two had been best friends. It was hardly as if you were startin' at the gate. Jax wants to blame you because he doesn't want to take responsibility for himself."

"He said it was both our faults. If I put too much into the relationship, he didn't put enough." She could tell she'd taken the wind out of the rest of Alice's speech. "But that doesn't change the fact that I'm falling into the same trap with Dev."

"It's hardly the same. He wanted to buy that place for you because he's committed."

"How do I know that? How do I know that he'll stick around? That the first time his family calls, he won't go running?"

Even as she said the words, she remembered him telling her that he loved her. That he was setting up his own business so his family didn't have leverage over him, so he could marry who he wanted.

"Caitlyn, do you hear yourself? What are you so afraid of? What do you have to lose?"

Everything. She had everything to lose. One bad experience with Jax and she'd become a cold fish. What would happen if she let Dev burrow even deeper into her heart than he already had?

"What do Dev and I really have? We've been playing a childish game where he pretended to humor me with boyfriend lessons." She spat out the last words, feeling ridiculous saying them out loud. "I don't want to repeat the mistakes I made with Jax. If it was real with Dev, he would've called me. Instead, one thing goes wrong and he's acting the exact same way as Jax."

"That's not fair, Caitlyn. It's really not the same situation."

"I'm done talking about this." She was done thinking about it, too. For two days she'd sat around the Lattimore mansion, moping. She'd started on this ill-thought-out endeavor with Dev because she was worried that Jax had ruined her for all men. Dev seemed to have brought out the sexual desire she thought she didn't have. But was it Dev, or had she finally conquered her demons? There was only one way to test her theory.

"Listen, I could use a night out. Do you want to go to the Lone Star?"

"Are you sure that's the best place for you to be right now?"

Caitlyn nodded. "I need to be someplace where I don't have to be myself."

Twelve

"I'm not sure this was a good idea." Alice grabbed her arm. Caitlyn shook it off. Whatever curse Jax had put on her had been broken, and she was determined to enjoy it. She'd managed to talk to half a dozen guys tonight, flirted, even danced with a couple of men. All without feeling the familiar tightness of panic in her chest. Maybe that's one thing Dev had been good for—being a practice boyfriend. That's all she had asked of him, after all.

"I'm not drunk, Alice. I'm perfectly in my senses and doing what you've been telling me to do for ages—letting loose."

The Lone Star was packed. It was a Friday night, and the smells of beer, peanuts and sawdust filled the air. The place was decorated like an Old West saloon with cowboy hats and horseshoes on the wall, a big, polished wood bar and a square dance floor. There was even a mechanical bull in one corner that was getting good use.

"Can I buy you a drink?"

Caitlyn turned to see a tall, muscular man with dark hair and thick eyebrows. He looked vaguely familiar, but Caitlyn couldn't remember where she'd seen him before. Alice placed a hand on Caitlyn's arm. She sighed. Alice was right. Partying all night wasn't Caitlyn's thing. She'd come here to test a theory, and she'd proven it. There was nothing wrong with her, never had been.

"I'm sorry, but…" She stopped. She didn't know what compelled her to, but her eyes suddenly went to the door. Her heart stopped in her chest. *How could he possibly be more handsome than I remember?* Dev walked in behind Russ wearing jeans that showed off his long legs and an untucked T-shirt. Hadn't he said Russ wanted him to come here to pick up women? Two days since they'd last spoken and he was already cutting his losses and moving on?

She tugged on her ear, a signal to Alice that she was happy to talk with the guy. They had a system. A tug on the ear for *go away, I am interested in this guy*, and a touch on the nose if she needed Alice to rescue her.

She turned to the handsome stranger and put a hand on his arm. "I'd love a drink. Beer will do."

He nodded and gestured to the bartender. It took Caitlyn and Alice the better part of half an hour when they'd ordered their drinks, but this guy had no trouble getting the female bartender's attention.

When they had their beers, she took a sip, then turned to him. "I'm Caitlyn," she said.

"Heath." Her pulse quickened. It couldn't possibly be the same Heath, could it?

"Yes, I am that Heath Thurston," he said, as if reading her mind.

"By that I assume you know I'm a Lattimore."

"The door isn't that far away, if you'd like to run."

Actually, what I'd like to do is throw this drink in your face. She took a breath and lifted her beer. "It's nice to meet you."

He clinked his beer mug with hers. "Mighty nice of you not to throw that in my face."

She smiled. "I considered it, but then I figure it's better to get you drunk and pump you for information."

He threw his head back and laughed. She snuck a look at Dev, who was staring right at them. A pleasant zing went through her at the murderous look in his eyes. She forced herself to turn back to the conversation with Heath. Perhaps she could find out more about his plans.

"It's nice to meet you, Caitlyn. I know I can't be very popular with your family right now."

"Yeah, they don't take kindly to having our home threatened."

Heath leaned over. "Listen, it's not my intention to cause chaos in your lives. I just want to do right by my sister's memory."

She nodded. "I can understand that."

"Tell me, Caitlyn, what is a beautiful girl like you doing in a place like this?"

His eyes sparked. He was flirting with her. She glanced at Dev, whose eyes were still fixated on her. Were her feelings for Dev real or just a rebound from Jax? Could she have the same chemistry with another man? Heath was certainly attractive enough.

"You think I'm beautiful?"

He smiled and she leaned forward, putting her elbow on the bar so their faces were barely an inch from each other.

"I think you're stunning."

"Well, you're not that bad yourself."

She leaned in farther, and mentally scanned her body for the heat and lust she should be feeling. Heath was devastatingly handsome. She hoped that the morning at the ranch with Dev had also unlocked the mental block her therapist claimed was her problem. Surely sitting this close to someone as handsome as Heath should have her as hot as bothered as one look at Dev.

Alas, she felt nothing.

Russ slapped Dev on the back. "You stare at her any longer, bud, and your face will freeze like that."

Dev rolled his eyes. The Lone Star was the last place he wanted to be, but Russ had insisted, and Dev didn't have the will left in him to fight. He'd spent the last two days wallowing in self-pity, asking himself how he could have misread the situation with Caitlyn. The first woman he'd fallen for and he'd managed to screw it up royally.

He glanced toward her again and caught her eye for just a second. She looked stunning in skintight jeans, a strappy red sequined top and high heels that made her entirely too sexy for a place like this. Why was she sitting so close to that guy? Why was she leaning into him as if she was going to kiss him? He clenched his fists. *That man better not lay a hand on her.* How could she let another man touch her? What did that guy have that he didn't?

Then it happened. The man kissed her. The bubble of anger that had been growing inside Dev boiled over. He stood and made his way to them. He pushed the man away from Caitlyn, breaking their kiss.

"Whoa, man! What the hell?" the man muttered.

"Dev!" Caitlyn screamed.

"What are you doing, Caitlyn?" Dev demanded.

"That is none of your business." Caitlyn said.

He looked daggers at the man who had been kissing the woman he loved. "Beat it."

"Listen, I don't want trouble, but it seems to me you're the one that should leave."

Dev glared at the man. He moved toward him, but Caitlyn grabbed his shoulder. "Dev, don't!"

He looked at her. Did she want to be with this loser? Had she already moved on from him? Had he just been a practice boyfriend all along so he could prepare her for the likes of this guy? She met his gaze, then sighed. "Heath, it was nice meeting you, but I need to talk to Dev."

She opened her purse to pay for the beer, but he waved her away. "Don't worry about it. Least I can do…considering."

She nodded.

Considering what? He wanted to ask her, but there were more important things on his mind. Like what was bar guy offering Caitlyn that Dev couldn't. *Royal.* The answer slammed into him. The man was from Royal. He could offer her the one thing Dev couldn't.

"Come on, Dev, let's find a quiet spot to talk. Just give me a sec." She turned to Alice, who was a few stools down on the bar, talking to a man, and whispered something to her. Alice turned to look at him for a beat, then nodded.

Each corner of the bar was louder than the last, so they decided to take the side exit and step into the alley. It was dark, lit only by the light spilling from the apartment building windows on either side. It smelled of tobacco smoke and something sweeter.

"What were you doing in there?" Even in the shadows, he could see the anger in her eyes.

"Me? What were you doing kissing that guy?"

"Excuse me? What's it your business who I kiss?"

He stepped back, the anger that had consumed him just moments ago replaced with a cold ice that seeped into his veins. Who was he indeed? "You know what, you're right." He shook his head. "I'm the crazy one. What was I thinking? All you wanted was a practice boyfriend, somebody to warm you up so you could go out with guys like him." He waved toward the bar door, then turned away from her.

"I guess you're done practicing with me."

Thirteen

The last thing Dev wanted to do was leave Caitlyn standing in the alley, but he'd already made his play. It was her turn now.

She made a strangled sound, and he closed his eyes. "Dev, don't go."

He hadn't even realized he'd been holding his breath until she said those words. He breathed out. She came around so she was facing him. "I need to tell you something."

That was not what he was expecting her to say. Especially not with that look of pain etched on her face. Instinctively, he put his hand on her shoulders. "Hey, are you okay?"

She nodded. "Can we go someplace and talk?"

It was getting late, and most of the Royal cafés

and restaurants were closed, so he drove in silence to his hotel. He was curious as to what she wanted to say, trying not to hope that she'd changed her mind. He handed his car key to the valet and directed her toward the hotel lobby.

She shook her head. "I want to talk someplace private. Can we go to your room?"

He sucked in a breath. "Caitlyn, are you sure?"

"Just to talk," she reiterated.

He shook his head. "I can't promise you that. I'll stick by what I told you on our first date. It'll be up to you when you want to move on from practicing, but being together in a hotel room is more than I can handle."

A pinkish tinge rose from her neck to her cheeks, and he tamped down on the heat that rose deep in his belly. She led the way to the elevator, and they went up to his room. When he'd checked in, all the suites were already taken, so he was in a standard room that had one large bed, a small desk and a little round table with two chairs.

It was hard to ignore the bed that took up most of the space, but he walked resolutely to the small table. "Let me order drinks from room service. Do you want something to eat?"

She shook her head. "Just coffee."

He ordered a pot and sat across from her. She bit her lip. He waited patiently.

"My best friend in high school was a boy named Jax. We never dated in high school, but there was always something between us. What I didn't know until just before Jax went off to college was that my father had paid for his tuition so that I'd have a friend. It broke my heart."

His heart lurched for her. She looked up at him, gauging his reaction. He gave her a small smile. "When I was in high school, I was a bit of a pimply-faced, chubby little boy."

That brought a smile out of her. "I have a hard time picturing that."

"I'll show you my parents' Facebook account which has documented my teenage years in embarrassing detail. Anyway, I did not secure a date to the school dance. My dad didn't want me to stand around alone all night. So, he hired an escort to take me to the dance, thinking I'd be the cool kid. Except half the geeks in the exclusive New York private school had the same idea and the escorts knew each other, so they ended up spending the night hanging out with each other while I stood in the corner."

The smile on her face was much bigger and more genuine, and it pinged his heart. He'd fallen hard for her. Would she break his heart?

He softened his voice. "I don't think my dad would intentionally try to hurt me, just like yours wouldn't. They're convinced that they know what's best for us. What they don't realize is that in trying to protect us, they hurt us even worse."

She blinked, and a tear rolled down her cheek. She looked so innocent and full of pain, his heart squeezed painfully. He wanted to reach over and brush the tear away. Instead he tentatively placed his hand on hers. He didn't want to move any closer and scare her away. There was more to the story, he could tell by the deep breath she took, and he wanted to give her the space she needed to tell it her way.

"Jax went away for college, and we didn't keep in touch. I was mad at him for keeping my father paying his tuition a secret. Then he came back to Royal and by then I'd forgiven him. We reconnected. He admitted that he had loved me all through high school, but his mother had warned him to stay away from me because she worked for my family. He wanted to know if I'd felt the same way, and of course I did. Jax had been my best friend for years. He knew me—I could talk to him. We already had feelings for each other. It made sense to explore whether what we had was deeper."

He nodded—he understood perfectly. He'd never met another woman with whom he connected the way he had with Caitlyn. With other women, when he told the story about the high school dance escort, they were horrified and what followed was a discussion about how inappropriate his parents were. How could he tolerate their intrusiveness? He'd never met an American woman who could understand why he still lived in his family home at the age of twenty-eight when he was gainfully employed and, in their words, "not a loser." Caitlyn hadn't asked him to explain any of these things when he'd told her.

"Our relationship moved pretty fast. In hindsight, I didn't bother to go through the steps. I was just so excited to get my old friend and high school crush back." Her voice cracked, and he squeezed her hand even as his own stomach roiled.

"Jax was my first. I've been with a few men since him, but it's all ended in the same way."

He felt the tremor running through her body and he longed to take her in his arms, but he didn't want to lose this moment. He sensed that what she was about to tell him would explain her behavior. There was no way that he was the only one who had been feeling their connection.

"Jax and I planned a special night. It wasn't his first time, but he knew it was mine, and he wanted it to be a good experience for me." She visibly swallowed. "I don't even know how to tell you what happened. I'm not sure I understand fully. Jax tried so hard to pleasure me, but it just wasn't working…for the both of us…" Her voice cracked again. "We tried again a few times, but it just got worse. He started having problems, too. When we broke up, he told me that he'd never had a problem being with a woman, but I was a…a cold fish."

She hung her head. How could any man be with Caitlyn and think of her as anything but the passionate woman she was? He wasn't sure if there was more to the story, but he also didn't want to scare her away by getting too close.

"I've spent months in therapy trying to figure out what's wrong with me. My therapist encouraged me to date, and I did. But the same thing has happened each time I've gotten close to a man. My therapist calls it a fear of intimacy."

"Caitlyn…"

"No, Dev, don't say anything. Don't tell me that I'm wrong or how I'm beautiful or that I turn you on. I've heard that before. The problem is not with you, it's with me."

You're wrong, Caitlyn. Just thinking about that morning in the barn aroused him. How responsive she'd been, how wet and hot her body got with his touch. Dev had been with enough women to know that there were different levels of attraction he himself felt with each partner, but not once did he question the red-hot chemistry Caitlyn ignited in him.

"The last time you and I met…at the ranch… I had bumped into Jax that day. He lives in Royal too but we have been studiously avoiding each other. He finally decided he was ready to talk. He said that I had put too much pressure on our relationship. We moved so quickly, going from old friends to a serious relationship in one step. It was too much too fast."

"Oh, Caitlyn." He squeezed her hand, at the same time aching for her and relieved to find out why she'd reacted the way she had. He had moved too fast, pushed her to make a commitment when she wasn't ready. He was doing exactly what Jax had accused her of doing.

He pushed his chair close to hers, cupped her face and wiped away her tears with his thumbs. "I'm sorry I put pressure on you, that I rushed things."

"I don't want the same thing to happen to us that happened with Jax."

He nodded. "I understand that, Caitlyn…and…"

A knock on the door interrupted him, and he swore under his breath. He'd forgotten about room service. He let the man in to set up the coffee service on the little table, glad that he'd thought to also order some cookies. Caitlyn looked a little pale and he wondered if she'd had dinner. The room service attendant poured the coffee while Dev signed the check, and then the man left.

Caitlyn automatically added cream to his coffee and sugar and cream to hers. They'd had coffee so often together she knew exactly how he liked his. With a twinge he thought about how lovely it would be to spend breakfast with her. But if there was anything their conversation had taught him, it was that he would lose her if he pushed too hard. She was running scared.

They finished their coffee in a comfortable silence, then he poured her another cup. "Caitlyn, I don't ever want you to feel like I'm pressuring you. I've never had a serious relationship like you had with Jax. You're the first woman that I feel like I've ever connected with. You get me. You know me. You understand me."

He couldn't read the expression on her face, and the coffee burned down his throat. Caitlyn was the first woman he'd loved and hadn't been afraid to tell. What she'd just told him solidified his feelings for her even more. He hadn't imagined their attraction, hadn't overestimated their chemistry or their connection. She felt what he did. But he also knew that there was only one way to convince her of that.

"But if friendship is all that you can give me, I understand, and accept."

Fourteen

Caitlyn stared at Dev. So, it was also happening with him. She'd admitted her deepest, darkest secret. The one only her therapist and Google knew about. What had she really expected? That he would take her into his arms and insist on proving her wrong? *Yes!*

She hadn't planning on telling him so much. But once she'd looked into his eyes, she'd realized that he was the only man who had ever told her he loved her and meant it. Jax had said "love you" once in a while, but it was in the way she said it to her siblings. He'd never told her he was in love with her.

Her brain screamed at her to call an Uber and go home. To save herself the humiliation that was sure to come. But she was frozen in her chair. He was looking at her expectantly, waiting for a response to his offer of friendship.

With every ounce of courage that she had, she stood. Her legs felt unsteady. Dev stood, too. "Caitlyn…"

"I have more than enough friends. I don't need another."

He stepped back, but she closed the distance between them. "What I need, Dev, is a lover. A man who can turn me on, who can show me that I'm not the passionless woman I think I am." His eyes widened, and she gave him a small smile. She stepped closer until she was well into his personal space.

Her legs felt like rubber. She wasn't sure how much longer she could stand. That's when his arm went around her, pulled her close. His head came down, and his lips seared onto hers. She met his kiss with a fervor of her own. Her body was on fire, and he was definitely aroused. She stepped back and lifted his shirt. He helped her get it off. She ran her hands across his muscular chest. He inhaled sharply, which spurred her on. She kissed his chest, ran her fingers over his nipples.

"I showed you mine, now you show me yours," he said cheekily and took off her shirt. She unclasped her bra, eager to feel her body naked and raw against his. He cupped her breasts and ran his thumbs over her nipples. She moaned, enjoying the feel of his hands on her. He bent his head and kissed the spot between her neck and shoulder, and her body pulsed with desire. She placed her hand on his erection, and his hardness made her even wetter than she was.

He wanted her. There was no awkwardness; she was enjoying his touch, not dreading it. In fact, she wanted—no, needed more of him.

She unbuckled his pants and slid them down, then kicked off her high heels and discarded her jeans and panties.

"Do you have a condom?"

He nodded and opened a drawer to retrieve it. He went to open the packet, but she stopped him. "Not quite yet." She smiled then pressed herself against him. She wanted to feel the full length of his naked body against her bare skin. He cupped her butt and lifted her up. She wrapped her legs around him and moaned as she felt him hard between her legs. He rubbed against her wet core and let out a guttural moan. Then he put his mouth to hers.

They were rubbing against each other, she hot and wet, he hard and strong. His shaft pressed against her clit, sending waves of ecstasy through her body. She wanted him so badly, she began writhing against him, inviting him to plunge inside her.

He walked them over to the bed and set her down. He took a deep breath, and she looked at him, taking in the fierceness of his erection. "Dev, please I need you inside me."

He shook his head. "Not quite yet." She hated that he was using her words against her. He put his mouth between her legs, and she lost it. His tongue flicked across her clit, then went in and out of her. His arms were beside her, and she grabbed onto them for support, bracing herself for the explosion about to go off inside her. She dug her fingers into his skin as he licked and sucked her. "Hmm, you taste amazing." He pressed his thumb against her clit as he flicked and sucked with his mouth, and she lost her mind. The pleasure that rocked through her body was sensational. She screamed and lifted her hips, and he cupped his mouth over her sex and sucked.

When she came down from her orgasm, her core was still throbbing. She grabbed his shaft and rubbed him against her clit. He moaned. "Caitlyn, oh my God, I can't hold out much longer." That just spurred her on even more. She grabbed and stroked him and could feel him pulsing in her hand. He stopped her, then quickly placed the condom on himself. When he entered her, she was sure she was going to shatter into a million pieces. He felt amazing inside her. She was already wet, but now her body molded itself to him, gripping his hard shaft as another orgasm pounded through her. She had wanted to do it with him, to finish the second time with him, but she couldn't wait. With her nails digging into his back, she tightened around him, giving in to raw, beautiful pleasure.

When she finally stopped pulsing, she noticed he had gone soft inside her. For a second, fear gripped her. Had it happened again? Had she managed to turn him off?

He smiled at her. "I'm sorry, I wanted to go a little longer, but I just couldn't hold off."

"You finished?" she asked shyly.

He pulled out of her and removed the condom. "A

little too soon for my liking, but we have all night for me to make it up to you."

He grinned at her.

"We do have all night? Don't we? You're not going to up and leave me again, are you?"

Caitlyn shook her head. There was no place she wanted to be other than in Dev's bed. She crawled under the sheets, and he joined her. She turned around so he could spoon her. Impossibly, he was hard again, but she wanted a moment to feel his body against her. To take a breath and process what had just happened. She'd seduced Dev, had made him hot for her, and he in turn had lit a fire in her body.

As they snuggled in together, she finally understood what her therapist had been trying to tell her. There really was nothing wrong with her. She needed to connect emotionally with a man to feel comfortable with the physical part of their relationship. That's why the kiss with Heath hadn't roused her, the way Dev did just by looking at her. She had opened up to him, shared herself with him and felt connected to him. Maybe she'd even fallen in love with him. The thought filled her with warmth, and she pressed close to him.

"Hmm, you keep doing that and I'm not going to be satisfied with just holding you."

She turned around to face him. He kissed her on the nose. "I wish you'd told me earlier about what happened with your ex. I can't believe that any man would think of you as cold. You are passionate, kind, caring…any man would be lucky to have you."

Her heart pinched. That day at the horse ring, he'd told her he loved her. Had his feelings changed? Had she managed to drive him away from her like she always did?

"I'm sorry for the way I reacted the other day when you suggested a business partnership."

He ran his hand down up and down her back, and her body responded immediately, involuntarily curving into him.

"I was just overwhelmed with the suddenness of the idea."

"Was it that or something else?"

There he was again, refusing to let her get away with the words she'd crafted. "What do you think it was? These days you seem to know me better than I know myself."

He smiled. "I doubt that." He pulled himself closer to her so his lips were almost touching hers. "But what I think is that you didn't like the fact that I was proposing a business relationship and not a personal one."

She shook her head. "That's crazy. We've only known each other for a few weeks—I wasn't expecting anything. You just took me by surprise, and I guess I didn't understand why you'd want to tie us together permanently without knowing where our personal relationship was going."

He kissed her briefly. "Where do you want it to go?"

She didn't hesitate. "You are my happily-ever-after, Dev. That's what I want."

"And where shall we live happily ever after?"

"In that ranch you found. We can make it a home. I can see some cozy farmhouse-style furniture, maybe curtains instead of the wood blinds that are there. I can take in horses and run my camp. You can see about turning that old Stevens brewery into your restaurant. You know, the more I think about it, maybe some remodeling could really make that place work. The location is so perfect, and…"

"Caitlyn," he interrupted gently. "You know I can't live my life in Royal."

She blinked. "I know. It was just a thought." He kissed her nose. "I'm not saying we can't come back here often to see your family, but my family business is based in New York, and if my restaurants are successful, I'll have to travel around."

She extricated herself from his arms and sat up. She'd known this conversation was coming and had been avoiding it. She hadn't had the words before, but now she understood why his plans for the ranch had bothered her so much. "What do you expect me to do? Stay by your side as we hop from one place to another? Or stay here in Royal, waiting for you to come home when your schedule allows?"

"I hadn't thought about it. We only just got together. Give us a chance, and we'll figure something out. My family has a private jet. We live in the same country. I have friends that make things work with partners in India—we'll find a way."

She wasn't sure she believed him. She wouldn't ask him to stay in Royal with her. He wouldn't be happy here. But she wasn't sure she could be happy anyplace else.

He ran a finger slowly from her lips, down her neck, between her breasts and down her legs. She was already wet and throbbing for him and more than happy to forget about the looming decisions between them. She had Dev right now, and his mouth was doing that thing he was so good at. She wasn't going to ruin it by thinking about the future. Tomorrow would come soon enough to ruin things.

Fifteen

When he opened his eyes, Caitlyn was next to him, naked and bathed in morning light. They'd had quite the night, finally falling asleep when the sun came up. He stared at her face, wondering how he was ever going to let her go. He was glad they'd put off having the conversation about the future last night. He hadn't wanted to ruin their first night together, but even after she'd fallen asleep, he'd stayed up thinking about what she'd said.

He couldn't ask her to follow him around while he set up his business. Nor could he move to Royal. While it was a charming town, it didn't feel like home for him. He'd seen his siblings give up their dreams for their spouses. He wouldn't do that, nor would he expect Caitlyn to do that for him. But he

was having a hard time finding a happy medium.
Wasn't he jumping the gun anyway? Caitlyn hadn't
even told him she loved him, and here he was trying
to figure out how to make their lives work together.

Caitlyn murmured something unintelligible, and
he kissed her forehead and left the bed. He checked
his phone to see what he had on the schedule and
cursed under his breath when he realized he had a
video call scheduled with his mother in a few minutes. He had overslept.

"What's got you lookin' like you got bit by a box
full of mosquitoes?"

He turned and smiled at her. She was sitting up
in bed, holding the white sheet to her chin, and he
loved her innocent smile and big eyes. This was the
Caitlyn he wanted to wake up to every morning—
rosy cheeked and looking at him like he was her
whole world.

"I guess you can't take the girl out of Texas." *Literally.*

She smiled. "No, you can't." She lifted an eyebrow toward the phone he was holding.

"I have a video call with my mom in five minutes."

The look of blissful pleasure on her face was replaced with panic. She scrambled out of the bed and
began looking for her clothes. "I need to get out of
here."

He stepped toward her and pulled her into his
arms. "No, you don't. I want you to meet my mom."

She shook her head. "Not looking like this, I can't.

And I need to prep, figure out what I'm going to say. I need to research some Hindi words and…"

He placed a finger on her lips. "No, you don't. You just need to be yourself, like you are with me. Don't put on the armor. It'll just be a quick hello."

"I still can't have her see me wearing your bed-sheet!"

He smirked. "Fine, put on clothes. It'll be nice to take them off again."

She gathered her clothes and raced into the bathroom just as his phone rang.

"Hi, Ma!"

"Dev, *beta*, how are you?"

They chatted for a few minutes. Dev tried to keep the video focused away from the bathroom door so he could properly introduce Caitlyn. His mother talked about the cuteness of his niece and then the latest drama of his siblings. Against his hopes, his brother had not really stepped up to help his father. His sister was handling things well, but things were falling apart at home for her. "It's time for you to come home, son. I don't want Maya's marriage to suffer because of the work she is doing for your father. I think he sees how capable she is and he'll give her more permanent responsibility."

Dev sighed. What his mother didn't know was that if Maya's marriage was suffering, it was because she was finally beginning to realize everything she'd given up for her husband. Her long-buried resentment was surfacing. He'd seen it since the day she quit her job. But now was not the time to discuss all that. He heard Caitlyn carefully opening the bathroom door and saw her peeking out. He waved her into the room. She'd pulled her hair back into a ponytail and washed her face. She looked incredible.

She gestured with her hands to leave but he shook his head.

"Why are you shaking your head?" his mother demanded. Caitlyn froze.

"Ma, you remember Caitlyn, whose picture I showed you? She's here, and I want her to say hello to you."

His mother immediately switched to Hindi, even though they'd been talking in English. "You know that is not how things are done. It is not proper to introduce me to a girl you are sleeping with."

"Ma, she's much more than that, and I think you know it. I wouldn't introduce you to someone unless I was serious about them."

His mother sucked in a breath. "Guess I have no choice but to meet her."

Caitlyn was already strapping on her heels. Before she could bolt, he gestured to her. "Ma, meet Caitlyn. Caitlyn, meet my mother."

Caitlyn glared at him quickly, then turned to face the camera and smiled.

"You are even prettier than the picture Dev showed me." His mother said.

He let out a breath. He didn't think his mother would be rude to Caitlyn, but she could be passive-aggressive.

Caitlyn smiled. "It is so nice to meet you, Mrs.

Mallik. I had hoped we would meet under better circumstances."

His mother smiled. "My son is known to be very inappropriate, but we shall cover for his inadequacies, shan't we."

Both Caitlyn and his mother smiled and continued to make small talk. His mother asked about her family, and, immediately at ease, Caitlyn told her all about them. They talked a little about the charities they were each involved in. His mother even took one of Caitlyn's suggestions for a children's charity.

He was glad to see Caitlyn at ease with his mother. He wanted them to get along, to know that Caitlyn could fit in with his family.

"Tell me, Caitlyn, do you identify as a Black woman or as a white woman?"

Dev sucked in a breath. At least his mother had asked diplomatically.

She smiled. "It's a great question. Until a couple of years ago, I would've said both. But the truth is, my family, the Lattimores, is Black, and whether I realized it or not, I've been treated like a Black woman most of my life."

"As a woman of color myself, I understand, my dear. So tell me, how will your children identify?"

"Excuse me?"

"It's something to think about, isn't it? Take my grand-daughter for example, beautiful child she is. My son married an Indian woman, but my granddaughter calls herself Indian American. When she makes little pictures of her family, she colors herself a different shade than her parents, even though she looks exactly like them."

He knew where his mother was going, and he wasn't going to let his mother sow doubt in Caitlyn's heart. "Well, we should get some breakfast, Ma, so I'm going to steal my girlfriend back."

"No, wait. I'd like to respond to that." Caitlyn took a breath. "There's no answer. All my life, I've felt like I didn't know how to describe myself. I wasn't white or Black. Personally, I think it's sad that we still define people by the color of their skin. I hope my children won't have to deal with that at school. But if they do, I'll tell them what my mother told me. *It doesn't matter. All I want is for you to love who you are.*"

"Your mother sounds like a good woman." Dev knew that tone in his mother's voice, and he was glad Caitlyn wouldn't recognize it for the condescension it was.

"It's time for us to go, Ma."

His mother switched back to Hindi. "Dev, she's a nice enough girl, but it doesn't change the fact that she's not Indian. It's time for you to come home and stop wasting your time in that backward Southern town." She hung up, and he took a breath to compose his face.

"She hated me, didn't she?" Caitlyn said quietly.

He shook his head. "No, she didn't hate you. She hates the fact that you're not Indian. That's something I'll work on with her." He tucked his phone away and cupped her face. "You did great."

"She has a point, you know."

"What do you mean?"

"What you wouldn't let her finish saying. That our backgrounds are very different. You don't know what it's like being Black, and I don't know what it's like to be Indian."

"So what, Caitlyn? How does that matter now? We have a lifetime to get to know each other's cultures and traditions."

She sat on the edge of the bed. "Until a couple of years ago, it wouldn't have mattered much to me, either. But one thing Jax made me see is how blind I'd been to the fact that I am Black, and that it affects how I see the world and how people treat me. It affects the responsibilities I have to my community as a member of the privileged class." She paused and swallowed. "It will affect how your family treats me."

"Listen, I've dated my fair share of Indian women, and let me tell you that what I value as a person is the same things you do. That's what's really important."

She shook her head. "Just now, your mom wanted to tell you what she thought of me, so she switched into a different language. That's how it'll always be. Your siblings married within your culture. I'll be an outsider in your family."

He sat beside her and took her hand. "I won't let that happen."

"Then you'll be an outsider in your own family."

He couldn't deny that she was right. It would take a long time for his family to get used to speaking

English at the dinner table. They'd made a pact to only speak Hindi at home to make sure the next generation, his nieces and nephews, learned their language. But surely that was a small thing to overcome.

He leaned over and kissed her cheek. "I'll teach you the language. Don't worry too much about it."

"I don't think it'll be that easy."

He shifted so he could cup her face and make her look at him. "No, it's not going to be easy. But you know what's nearly impossible? Finding that one person who gets you and supports you and will be there for you. What we have is worth fighting for." He gazed at her. "I've been with my fair share of women, and the connection we have, it's nothing like I've had before. In my culture, we believe that there is one person who is made for us, our soul mate. You're mine, Caitlyn, and I'm willing to do whatever it takes to make it work."

Her eyes shone. "Are you sure, Dev? I know how much your family means to you. I don't want to be the one that comes between you and them."

He kissed her briefly on the lips. "You won't."

She turned her face and kissed his hand. "As long as you stand by my side, we'll face it together. My family won't be that easy, either."

"Is it because I don't speak with a Texas twang?"

She smiled. "Yes, and you're not a rancher, and you're not from Royal."

"That's a problem for you, too, isn't it? That I'm not from Royal."

She took his hands in hers. "I love you, Dev. I

think I've loved you since the moment I spit my wine in your face."

A feeling of warmth and relief flooded through him. "I love you, too, Caitlyn. I promise you, we will figure it out. Finding love, that's impossible. Figuring out where to live and how to make a business work, that's just logistics."

"You make it sound so easy."

She leaned over and kissed him, and he kissed her back. A slow, sweet kiss to let her know that he loved her and that he was willing to fight for them.

"How about we spend the rest of the day together, forget about our families and just enjoy the fact that we have each other?"

She nodded. "Can we start by ordering breakfast? I'm famished."

He bent his head and kissed the spot between her neck and shoulder that made her break out in goose bumps. "Can I feast on something else first before we start breakfast?"

She murmured her approval and took off his shirt. He happily obliged and took off his jeans as she shed her own clothes. He wanted to take his time, but she had other ideas. As soon as his clothes were off, she grabbed his erection. Her hands were soft but her touch firm, and he nearly lost it. How could it be that her merest touch set his body on fire? He was usually much more reserved, but found it hard to hold himself back with her.

"Caitlyn, one second…"

She shook her head. "I don't want to take it slow. I want you now."

The fire in her eyes matched the one burning through his body. He knew what this was about. The conversation with his mother had deflated the bubble they'd created around themselves last night, believing that a declaration of love was all they needed. They both needed an immediate and urgent reminder that it was real between them, and that it was worth it. Or perhaps he was the one who needed reminding. He couldn't admit it to her, but she was right about the fact that it wouldn't be easy with his family and he'd have to give up part of his own relationship with them to be with her. He needed to be strong. His family always had a way of pulling him back in, of sucking him into their fold and their needs. What he needed was Caitlyn.

She pulled his arm with one hand while the other stayed firmly on his impossibly hard shaft. She lay back on the bed and guided him inside her. She was slick and he tried to tell her to take it slow, but she wouldn't listen, arching her hips to take him deeper inside her. Somewhere a phone rang, but he ignored it. He kissed her and she moaned, moving her hips. He matched her movements, feeling her tighten around him. The sensation was too much for him, but he held on as long as he could, determined to make sure she finished before he did, though it was hard to hold on with her tight around him and moaning with pleasure. She lifted her hips as her orgasm took over, and he couldn't hold himself back as she vibrated and pulsed against him.

"What's that ringing?"

He registered the same phone ringing that he'd noted when they got started, but where was it coming from? It wasn't his cell.

"That's my cell phone," she exclaimed.

The ringing stopped and she relaxed against him, but a minute later, it rang again. He slid out of her, seeing the panic on her face.

"I better get it, make sure it's not an emergency."

She scrambled out of bed, and he smacked himself. He'd forgotten the condom. How could he have been so stupid and not protected her? He knew he was healthy and didn't doubt for a second that she was, too, but he should've been more responsible. He'd gotten caught up in the moment and lost his mind. He'd have to tell her, make sure she took whatever precautions she needed to. How would she react when he told her? If this had happened with any other woman, he would've been freaking out. Actually, this would never have happened with another woman. But if it had to happen, he was glad it was with Caitlyn.

She answered the phone. "Sorry, I wasn't near my phone." She was breathless. "I'm on my way. I'll be there in fifteen minutes."

She looked at him as she clicked End on her phone. He was already pulling on his clothes. "What's wrong?"

"The private investigator found something about the claim on our ranch. The Grandins are coming over—the whole family is gathered. I need to go."

Sixteen

"I'll drive you."

Caitlyn sighed. Was she ready to bring Dev into her family fold? The Grandins were like family. If she took Dev with her, he'd meet all of them. *What if they don't like him? What if they scare him off?*

She pulled on her jeans and checked her appearance in the mirror. She couldn't show up looking like she was doing the walk of shame. Even though she was.

"I don't have to meet them. I can just drop you off."

She looked at him as he was fixing his own appearance. He pulled on a fresh shirt and ran a comb through his hair. There was a five o'clock shadow on his face, but he managed to make it look like it belonged there.

"Caitlyn, I need to tell you something."

She turned to him, her stomach clenching at the hollowness of voice. *What's wrong now?*

He swallowed. "I'm so sorry, I forgot to put on the condom that last time."

She almost laughed. How could she have forgotten? She was so careful. Almost without thinking, she looked at her phone for the date. *Crap.* Of course it was the time of the month when she should be even more careful.

"I take full responsibility. I know we have to go now, but I want you to know that I will be there for you, that…"

She put a finger on his lips. "The responsibility was as much mine as it was yours. If something happens, we will figure it out together."

He gave her a quick kiss, and all she had to do was look in his eyes to know that he was all in with her. He'd introduced her to his mother. While he made it out to be no big deal, she knew it was. It was clear from the overly casual way his mother had asked her some pretty deep questions about her family. The very fact that his mother had known about her before she and Dev had even slept together meant his feelings were serious. If he could take a gamble on her, she needed to make the same commitment to him.

"I want you to meet my family. There's no time like the present." Plus, she knew her family would be better behaved in front of the Grandins.

He placed his hands on her shoulders, forcing her to look up at him. "You don't have to, Caitlyn. I want to meet your family when you're ready. I'm in no rush."

She smiled. "Let's do it."

When they arrived at the Lattimore mansion, her family was gathered in the living room. All eyes turned to them as they walked in. Her grandfather Augustus was sitting in the large wing-back chair that was his spot in the family room.

Every time she saw her grandfather, it was hard to believe that he wasn't the same person he used to be. While he was still the tall, physically imposing figure she remembered from her childhood, his mind was not what it used to be. Her grandmother Hazel sat with Caitlyn's father, Ben, and her mother, Barbara. There was an antique silver pot on the coffee table, which she knew held the special brew coffee that her grandparents liked. Royal Doulton teacups, the service set from her parents' wedding, were set out along with little sandwiches, scones and pastries. Caitlyn's stomach rumbled, and she remembered they hadn't eaten breakfast.

Jayden was sitting opposite her parents, but Jonathan was pacing behind the couch. Their living room held three grand sofas and several chairs.

She was holding Dev's hand, and he squeezed it as a silence fell over the room. Caitlyn straightened, trying to stand as tall as she could. "Hi, everyone. This is my...this is Dev." *Boyfriend* seemed like the wrong word for him. Jax had been her boyfriend. Dev was so much more.

Jonathan was the first to speak. He made his way toward them. "Welcome, Dev." He held out a hand, and Dev shook it.

Before anyone else had a chance to speak, the Grandins arrived. Victor Jr. was accompanied by his son Vic, and his daughters Chelsea and Layla. Their younger sister, Morgan, hadn't come. Layla's fiancé, Josh, was there, and for once Caitlyn didn't feel the ping of jealousy that she did when she saw them. They all greeted each other, and everyone gave Dev a not-too-subtle once-over.

Layla sidled up to Caitlyn when she was alone for a second. "Who is that handsome stranger with you?"

"Someone I care about," she answered honestly.

"Well, whoever he is, hold on to him." Layla winked at Caitlyn, then went to help herself to the refreshments.

Dev handed Caitlyn a cup of coffee with some pastries on the saucer. "Why don't you sit and have something to eat?"

"Could you hear my stomach grumbling?"

He smiled. "I have a feeling you're going to need your strength for this meeting."

She had no doubt. Usually when the Lattimores and Grandins got together, there was chatter and merriment, but today, everyone found a seat pretty efficiently, many forgoing food or coffee.

Jonathan placed a large speaker in the center of the coffee table. It looked like an octopus, with cables that connected to multiple mini speakers that he spread out. It was the conference room telephone. "I have the private investigator, Jonas Shaw, and Alexa on the line."

Caitlyn had never seen everyone so quiet. She and Dev had chosen to stand behind the couch where her parents were seated. Her hand trembled slightly, and she set her cup on a side table. Dev handed her a small scone from his own plate, but she shook her head. Her appetite had vanished. He took her hand and squeezed it.

Jonas Shaw's voice was deep and crackly over the speakerphone. "I know you folks are anxious to know what I found, so I'll get right to it."

The room stopped breathing, but all Caitlyn could think about was the secure feeling of Dev's hand on hers. What if she found out in two weeks that she was pregnant? How would she feel? *Why aren't I freaking out about it?* Was she crazy to believe that he was committed to her?

Jonas cleared his throat. "As y'all know, Ashley Thurston was born about nine months after Daniel Grandin had an affair with Cynthia Thurston. You guys hired me to investigate the legitimacy of the papers that Heath Thurston is using to claim the oil underneath both your lands. I found a lawyer that used to work here in Royal. He's long dead now, but his daughter had his old papers. I went through them and found a copy of the paper Heath Thurston has."

The room took a collective breath. Until now, their entire strategy had been to refute the authenticity of the papers Heath Thurston had produced with Victor Sr. and Augustus's signatures.

"What about Augustus's signature on those papers?" her father asked.

"I'm afraid that's more bad news. Among the lawyer's papers was a logbook. Each person who visited the office signed in. On the day the papers were signed, Augustus's name was in the log, along with his signature. The same signature that was on the papers."

Silence hung like dead weight in the room, then Alexa spoke up. "Did you check to see if Augustus could have been there for other business? Maybe he was using the lawyer for something else?"

Caitlyn hated that they talked about her grandfather like he wasn't in the room. She looked at Augustus. The scowl on his face suggested he didn't like it, either.

"I checked, but I couldn't find anything related to Augustus. I reviewed the logbook for the month before and after, and Augustus didn't go to the office on any of the other days. Looks like his signature is legit."

Alexa and Layla asked Shaw several more questions, trying to find a way to dispute the information he was giving them, but it was of no use. It was pretty clear that Heath Thurston's claim was real and both of their ranches were in danger. Once Jonas had hung up, her father turned to her grandfather.

"Daddy, do you remember Victor asking you to sign something?"

Augustus frowned at his son. "Why are you askin' me? And who was that on the phone besmirching my name? Why don't you ask Victor? Where is Victor anyway?"

Her grandmother stood and placed a hand on Augustus's shoulder. "Darlin, Victor can't be here right now."

"Then I'm not staying, either." Her grandfather rose from the chair, surprisingly agile for his age.

"I think I better take him back to bed," Hazel said.

When they'd left, everyone began talking at once.

"Augustus had no right to sign over our land to pay for Daniel's sins," Ben grumbled. Caitlyn had never seen her father so riled up.

"Excuse me, but how do we know that your father isn't the one that put my grandfather up to this?" Chelsea exclaimed, tucking her long, flowing hair behind her ear. As the eldest daughter of the Grandin clan, Chelsea was fearless, and not afraid of butting heads with anyone.

Jonathan spoke up, his tone sharp and cutting. "Augustus isn't the one who had an affair and a child out of wedlock."

Caitlyn noted the fear and anger on the faces around the room. Their families had been friends forever, and they were turning on each other.

Layla chimed in. "I don't for a second—"

"Everyone stop!" Caitlyn cut in, surprised at the strength in her voice. Since she rarely spoke, everyone turned in surprise.

She made eye contact with everyone. "Now is not

the time to turn on each other. Our only hope in getting through this is to work together. Both our properties are at risk here."

Alexa's voice crackled over the phone. "Only if there is oil. What if we can prove there isn't?"

Heads all around the room started nodding, obviously liking Alexa's line of thinking.

Victor Grandin Jr. spoke up. "I'll get Jonas working on that." He picked up his phone and left the room to make the call.

"It seems to me that what we need is a good lawyer," Caitlyn stated. "Our current ones don't have the personal investment we need to make sure this goes our way."

She didn't have to say more. All eyes turned to the phone.

"Alexa, we need you and your brilliant mind," Layla said softly.

"I know you weren't plannin' on coming home soon, honey, but this is too important," her mother said.

Alexa sighed. "I'll represent us on this. Caitlyn is right. We have to work together. Right now the most important thing is that no one from either of our families has any contact with Heath or Nolan Thurston. Is that understood?"

Caitlyn tensed and gave Dev a sideways glance. He didn't know that the man in the bar last night had been Heath Thurston.

"We don't know what the brothers' next steps are,

and what we don't want is to inadvertently give them information that helps their case," Alexa continued.

Everyone nodded solemnly even though Alexa couldn't see them. Barbara invited the Grandins to stay for brunch, but everyone seemed to have lost their appetite. The Grandins rose to leave.

"I think I should go," Dev whispered to Caitlyn as everyone said goodbye to each other.

She grabbed his hand. "Don't."

He shook his head. "I think you need to focus on your family right now. There will be plenty of time for them to get to know me. Right now, they need you to process the news they just got, and you need to be here for them."

She smiled at him, unwilling to let him go but loving him for being so considerate and understanding that her family needed her. "I'm sorry about our day together."

"There will be plenty more." He gave her a chaste kiss on the cheek, then slipped out quietly.

"Where'd your fella go?" her father said as he poured himself a cup of coffee from the fresh pot that one of the kitchen staff brought out.

"This wasn't the best time to bring him," Caitlyn said.

"There's never a good time," Jonathan said gruffly. Her brother was sporting his signature jeans, T-shirt and cowboy boots. "I kinda wanted to talk to the guy."

"What, so you could get his social security number?" Jayden piped up. He picked up a sandwich and tossed it in his mouth, much to his mother's chagrin. She handed him a plate, and he promptly set it down.

"Have you been researching him?" Caitlyn could see her brothers cyberstalking Dev. "Did Alexa tell you about him?"

"Relax, sis. He seems like a solid guy." Jayden said.

Jonathan cleared her throat. "I still have some questions I'd like to ask him."

Caitlyn shook her head. "This is why I didn't want him sticking around."

"Caitlyn, did you know that his siblings are both married to people from their culture?"

"Yes, Jonathan, I know that. I don't see what that has to do with me dating him."

"Oh, Caitlyn, darlin', I could see clear as day that you two are in love with each other. You'd never have brought him today if you weren't serious about him." Her mother patted the seat next to her, and Caitlyn went to her.

"Why do I feel like you're all ganging up on me?"

Her mother put an arm around her. "We just want to make sure you know what you're doing."

"I'm not a child, and for your information, he introduced me to his mother today."

"And how did that go?"

"It went fine."

"Has Dev talked to you about whether his family is willing to accept someone outside their culture?" Her father put a sandwich on a plate and handed it to her.

"Are you guys willing to accept him? He's not Black." She set the plate on a side table. Her stomach was churning, and she couldn't imagine eating.

"You know that doesn't matter to us," her mother said.

"There's no point in talking about this when we don't know anything about his family. We've barely known each other for three weeks. Aren't you all always on my case about getting out more and dating and getting over Jax? Well, how am I supposed to do that when the first man I bring home gets the Texas inquisition?"

Her siblings had the courtesy to look sheepish. Alexa called out and everyone suddenly remembered she was still on the phone. In her take charge voice, she asked everyone to sit down so they could discuss what their next steps should be. Only Alexa could command a room even when she wasn't in it. After a while, Caitlyn stood, grabbed the plate her father had given her, loaded it up with sandwiches and left. Talking to death about what lay ahead wouldn't change the situation. One thing hit her with certainty—she wouldn't be able to open her camp on the Lattimore property anytime soon. The legal machinations Alexa was talking about would take forever, and Caitlyn couldn't keep putting her camp on hold for that long.

Then another thought punched her in the gut. Dev was supposed to be leaving town today, and not once had he mentioned staying.

Seventeen

Caitlyn breathed a sigh of relief when Dev texted to ask if he could pick her up a few hours later. She had already washed her hair and blown it out. She went to one of her favorite boutiques in town and, much to the amusement of the shopkeeper, picked out a red dress that was unlike anything she owned. The neckline was scandalous, and that's exactly what she wanted. She wore it without a bra, as it was meant to be worn. The dress cupped her breasts and tied in the back, then came around the front of her body like a wrap and ended in a bow.

She shivered with excitement at the thought of Dev loosening that bow and unwrapping the dress from her. She wore it with a pair of strappy heels and a new silk thong. She closed her eyes and imagined

Dev's hand on that thong, and her core throbbed with anticipation. As she looked at herself in the mirror, she barely recognized the woman in front of her. Her cheeks were flushed, her skin glowed and the dress looked like it belonged on the cover of a fashion magazine.

She was ready just as Dev pulled to the front of the house, which was eerily quiet after the drama of the morning. Dev exited the car to open the door for her and looked at her quizzically. "Isn't it a little hot to be wearing a coat?"

She gave him a smile, then looked around to make sure there were no staff or siblings lurking nearby. She took off the raincoat she'd thrown on and twirled for him.

Dev whistled appreciatively.

"I can't be seen wearing something like this. I bought it just for you."

He touched her partially bare back and kissed her on the cheek. "You look sensational," he breathed into her ear, and her heart fluttered at the hungry look in his eyes. He looked back toward the front door of her house. "Any chance your family is gone? I don't think I can drive with you looking like that."

She shook her head, smiling. He sighed and got into the driver's seat. "I was going to take you out to dinner, but I'm not sure I can share you with anyone else tonight."

"There is no way I'm going out on the town looking like this. I have a reputation as a stuffy Lattimore to keep up. This dress is just for you."

The wolfish smile he gave her and the dark hunger in his eyes made the dress totally worthwhile.

"Why don't you drive to the corner of Main and Porterhouse? My favorite Italian restaurant is there, and we can get some takeout. I'll place the order now and it'll be ready by the time we get there."

Once they picked up the food, he turned down Porterhouse Street. "Wait, the hotel is on the other side."

He smiled. "We're not going to the hotel. Just wait and see."

He pulled up to one of the new condo buildings that had been built at the edge of town. He turned to her. "I rented a place here. Didn't feel right to keep taking you to a hotel room."

She refused to think about what that meant. He'd rented a place. That was a sign that he wasn't leaving anytime soon.

The condo he'd rented was on the top floor of the building with a great view of the neighboring ranches. The space was light and airy without being ostentatious. There was an open kitchen, living room, dining room and two bedrooms. It was sparsely furnished with basic but tastefully modern furniture.

"How did you get it set up so quickly?" It had only been a few hours since she'd last seen him.

"Well, I only had a suitcase to move. The place was already furnished and ready to rent."

He stepped behind her and circled his arms

around her. He kissed the back of her neck, and a shiver of anticipation zinged through her.

"It definitely needs some homey touches. Maybe you'd be willing to help?"

Setting up house with you? Sign me up!

"So you plan to stay in Royal?"

"For now."

There was that maddeningly unclear answer. *What does* for now *mean?* Before she had a chance to ask, he trailed kisses down her neck and to the bare spots on her back. He cupped her breasts and moved his thumbs over her nipples, and all thought left her mind as heat flooded her body.

"Now, how do I unwrap this dress and get to my present?"

She undid the bow in the front of the dress, her body electrified with the anticipation of what was coming.

Suddenly the doorbell rang. Dev cursed under his breath, and she looked at him quizzically. "Expecting someone?"

He adjusted his pants and yelled, "Coming." She began rewrapping the dress. "My mom said that she was sending a package, so I told the hotel to send the courier over here when it arrived. I assumed they would leave it by the front desk."

When her dress was rewrapped, Dev went to answer the door, and Caitlyn moved out of view. She didn't want anyone seeing her in that dress, even if it was just a courier.

"Dad, what are you doing here?"

Wait what? Who!

"Surprise!"

This was not happening to her. Pulse racing, Caitlyn looked for the raincoat and realized it was on the other side of the room. She couldn't get to it without crossing in front of the door and being seen. Would it be better to hide in the bedroom until Dev's father left? Hiding was not a good idea. With her luck, he would decide to stay the night and then it would look even worse for her to be caught in the bedroom.

The man who entered the apartment looked nothing like Dev. He was half a foot shorter and lean, with thinning hair and round glasses. Despite the heat, he was dressed in a business suit. Regardless of his small size, he had a booming voice, and Caitlyn could see Dev shrinking right in front of him.

"Your mother was worried about you. I came to take you back to New York with me. Our jet is at the airport. Things are…" He stopped when he caught sight of Caitlyn.

"Ah, I see you have company." He eyed Caitlyn, and she shrank back, wishing she had hidden in the bedroom. "Sorry, I should have called. I can come back."

"No, it's okay, Dad. I want to—"

"No, no, son. You paid for the night, you should enjoy yourself."

It was as if someone had seared her with a branding iron. She raced to the kitchen to collect her coat, threw it on and picked up her purse. She couldn't stay one more second. This was not the way to meet Dev's father. "I need to go," she mumbled.

"Caitlyn, wait, no, don't leave." Dev caught her hand as she tried to race past him and put an arm around her. "Dad, this is Caitlyn, my girlfriend."

Her father's eyebrows shot up. "I see why your mother is worried," he said.

"Dad! Don't be rude. Caitlyn is important to me."

"No, it's okay, this is not the right way for us to meet. I'm sorry." She pushed Dev aside, wanting nothing more than for the floor to open up and swallow her whole.

"Let me drive you home."

She met his gaze, her eyes pleading. She couldn't take any more embarrassment. She shook her head, "Dev, please, take care of your dad. I need to go. I'll take an Uber." She turned on her heels and left.

"Dad, you can't just show up like that."

"Why not? Because you're ashamed? And what is this about you moving from the hotel and leasing an apartment? I thought you were here to open a restaurant. Where is the restaurant? What have you been doing?"

Dev took a breath. He knew things looked bad from where his father stood. He was a traditional Indian man, and it was bad enough that his first introduction to Caitlyn had been in his apartment, but to have her dressed as she had been was a double whammy. He needed to calm the situation before things really got out of hand.

"Dad, let's start over. Why don't you come and sit? Let me get you a glass of water and then we can talk."

Temporarily mollified, his dad took a seat at the glass dining room table. Dev eyed Caitlyn's dinner favorites and sighed. He handed his father a glass of water, then plated the food for both of them. It was a practice in his father's business to serve tea and refreshments before every meeting. It irritated Dev, who considered it a waste of time and money, but his father had a saying that rhymed in their language. Translated, it meant that if stomachs are empty, words are, too. It's how business was done in India, and it went beyond hospitality. He hoped this time, it reduced his father's crankiness.

"*Beta*, I came to take you back."

"Dad, I told you when I left that I need to chart my own course."

"I understand that. I did the same thing when I was your age. Your grandfather was dead set against me coming to America. He even refused to pay for my ticket. Your mother and I came here with nothing. We stayed with relatives, and I used my savings and sold your mother's jewelry to buy my first business. From that I built up an entire empire. I understand your need to be your own man, and I want to support you."

There was a big *but* coming, Dev could feel it, and he braced himself.

"And I will support you, *beta*. But I need your support right now." His father sighed, took off his glasses and rubbed the bridge of his nose. All his life, his father had seemed larger than life. The great Vishvanath Mallik, the man who reduced competitors to tears after filling them full of tea and mini cucumber sandwiches. Right now, all Dev saw was how shrunken his father looked, and the bags under his eyes.

"I know you have pushed me to consider your sister and brother to run the business. What you don't know is that I have given your brother, Khushal, several chances. He likes the lifestyle but not the work. Your sister, Maya, is very capable, but this job comes at a cost. You know that her in-laws are old and live with them. The last three weeks that you've been gone, her marriage has suffered. Her husband has told her in no uncertain terms that she can't keep working the hours she's been working. Their household is falling apart. That's why I'm here. I had hoped to handle things without you, give you a chance to pursue your own dreams, but I'm getting to be an old man now. I can't handle it all. I need your help."

Dev's stomach knotted. "Dad, I've told you that we need to hire more executives. You have to trust people outside the immediate family."

"You haven't lived like I have, son. You don't know how vulnerable family enterprises like ours are. One mistake and the entire business can fall. I told you how your uncle inherited my father's factories in India. I was so busy running things in America that I trusted him to run the factories that were my inheritance. He ran them into the ground. Factories that your great-grandfather built under the British rule, when hardly any Indians were allowed to own property and have wealth. Those factories survived colonialism and crumbled because of some bad decisions. I can't trust someone else."

It was an argument that he and his father had been having since Dev had graduated from business school. He'd felt totally unprepared to be the CFO and COO of this father's company as a new graduate, but his father had never been convinced to hire someone for those roles.

"Dad, Maya is a grown woman. Don't you think she should make her own decisions? She loves working—she went to Harvard Business School. When I don't know how to handle something, I call her."

"Her husband came to me directly, and I promised him that I'd bring you back so Maya could return her attention to their marriage."

"Don't you think that's unfair of Neeraj? I've only been gone for three weeks, and he's already coming to you. He, and you, haven't even given Maya a chance."

"Dev, this is not up for debate. You know how your mother and I feel about marriage. We wouldn't have what we do if it weren't for your mother. Maya has the same responsibilities to her family."

"Aren't we her family, Dad?"

"Once married, a woman's priority is the family she marries into."

"Dad, the world has changed, and we aren't

in India anymore. You have to give up these old-fashioned beliefs."

"Does this have to do with that girl?"

Dev straightened. "No, Dad, this is much bigger than Caitlyn alone…"

"Because if it is, let me tell you that your mother and I are not going to let you throw your life away on a girl like that."

Dev dug his nails into his hands, trying to formulate his anger into a respectful sentence. "You don't know Caitlyn. What you walked into today was a private romantic moment."

"Look, Dev, I know you think me old-fashioned, but I'm not that traditional. Maya dated, and I don't expect your future wife to be pure and virginal, but I do expect her to have some decorum, family values and…"

"Caitlyn has all that and more in spades. Like I said, you caught her at a bad moment, but she comes from one of the most respectable families in Texas. She herself is on the board of the local hospital and several charities. She tirelessly supports her family every—"

"Your mother told me all about Caitlyn. The issue is not whether her family is respectable enough and if she herself has good values. It's whether she is willing to leave her family to come support you and your dreams. Your life is in New York. Will she leave her life in Royal to come be with you?"

Dev's mouth went dry. *No, she won't.*

Eighteen

Caitlyn turned off the phone so it would stop buzzing. It was Alice, who had heard from Russ, who had shown up to Dev's new digs to find his father there. Dev had not texted or called. She knew he needed time to talk to his dad and smooth things over, but it had been more than six hours since she'd left his place. Caitlyn couldn't shake the feeling that things were not going well with his dad.

Worse, she couldn't help wondering if his father had succeeded in doing what she feared most. Had he convinced Dev to go back to New York? To give up on Caitlyn?

It was late into the night and she was exhausted. She checked her phone again. No calls from Dev.

She turned off the phone and tucked herself into bed. There was nothing she could do tonight.

She slept fitfully. This time she dreamed that she was naked in bed with Dev and the Lattimores and Grandins all walked in on them and accused her of colluding with Heath Thurston. She woke up in a cold sweat and realized it was only 4:00 a.m. She checked her phone and cursed under her breath when she saw ten missed calls from Dev. He'd called right after she fell asleep.

Unable to return to sleep, she opened her laptop and pulled up the listing for the ranch Dev had wanted to buy with her. Her stomach clenched when she saw "under contract" on the listing. Someone had put an offer on the place. She slammed the laptop shut. It was a sign that she and Dev weren't meant to be. She'd planned to buy the place and surprise Dev with it, but clearly fate was also shitting on them.

It was too early to go riding. She didn't want to show up at the barns and screw up the morning chore schedule. She decided to go for a swim.

After a few laps, Caitlyn heard Alexa as she came up for a breath.

"You training for the Olympic team?"

Caitlyn propped herself on the edge of the pool where Alexa was standing. "Woke up early. It's too hot to run and too early to ride."

Alexa was in jeans, a loose t-shirt and carried a paper cup.

"You took the early morning plane from Miami?"

Alexa nodded. "I need to review all the family papers and whatever Jonas found."

"I know this whole legal business is horrible but the silver lining is that you'll be home more now."

Alexa tilted her head. "What's going on, Caitlyn? You only swim like that when you're upset. What's wrong?"

She bit her lip. The last thing she needed was Alexa's judgment. "Any more news after the bombshell yesterday?" Had that only been yesterday? She still couldn't believe how much had happened in one day. She'd gone from waking up to the promise of a new life with Dev to having the rug pulled from underneath her. In all that, she hadn't even stopped to think about what the call with Jonas Shaw meant for their family's future.

"No real new information, but what Jonas found is pretty damning for us. We need to figure out what Heath Thurston wants out of all of this, but we also need to be careful about how we approach him and Nolan."

"I know it was my idea, but are you really okay with taking this on?"

Alexa shrugged. "I have been thinking about this since it happened. This is too important to trust to an outsider. But I can't stay in Royal. My life is in Miami. I'm going to need your help." She took a breath. "Caitlyn, the family is going to need you in the coming months. This fight with the Thurstons is going to be tough. And Grandpa is getting worse. Dad tried talking to him alone yesterday, and he doesn't remember what he may or may not have signed."

Caitlyn took a breath. "What do you need help with?"

Alexa smiled. "We all know how much you do for the family, and we appreciate it. I'm counting on you to help me fight this claim. I can only stay for a short time. Can you help me with sorting through Grandpa's papers?"

Caitlyn smiled and nodded. Maybe it was a good thing that the little ranch had sold. Her place was right here with her family. They needed her. She exited the pool and got dressed, opting for the most conservative clothes she had, which was most of her closet. Despite the heat, she settled for a pantsuit with a white collared shirt. She added her pearls and drove into town to her favorite bakery. She'd called ahead for an order of coffee and pastries. When they'd come to Dev's rental condo the previous day, he'd put her name on the list with the front desk so she could get a spare key anytime. Dev tended to sleep a little later, so she picked up the key in case he didn't answer her knock. She hoped she was early enough to offer them breakfast. Though what had happened the day before was tough to overcome, she owed it to their relationship to talk to Dev face-to-face.

She knocked on the door, but there was no answer. She used the key to enter. The place looked exactly as it had yesterday, but something was amiss. She set breakfast on the counter and noticed both bedroom doors were open.

She walked to the first door, her legs rubbery. The bedroom was pristine. The bed looked like it hadn't been slept in. She peeked in the second bedroom, and it looked the same. Had Dev and his dad woken up really early? Something about the tight corners of the bedsheets bothered her. She doubted that Dev, who had grown up with household staff, could make the beds so well. She walked into the room and threw open the closet door. She raced into the other room and found the same thing. She looked in every corner of the condo.

Dev was gone.

Nineteen

Dev cursed at his phone when he woke. His wireless charger hadn't quite connected, so the phone hadn't charged and was now dead. He placed it on the charger again and went to get dressed. His parents owned a penthouse triplex on the east side of Central Park. His room was palatial by any standards but especially New York City standards—it held a king-size bed, his exercise equipment, a deluxe desk decked out with all the technology he could ever want and an en suite bathroom. Looking around the room he realized just how frat boyish it looked with his clothes from last night on the floor and the dark leather furniture. He made a mental note to ask his mother to call the decorator to redesign the room. He walked into the shower and let the ten body jets and rain shower wake him up. He hated waking up this early.

After arguing with his father for hours, he'd finally agreed to get on the family jet and come home for a few days. He'd called Caitlyn multiple times, but she hadn't answered. It was too complex to leave a voice mail. He'd just keep trying. He didn't want to leave things the way they were, but after talking with his father he'd realized that he had to come home and deal with whatever was going on with Maya. He was her older brother and had always protected her.

His phone was ringing when he exited the shower. It was his sister, Maya, calling to tell him that she was in the dining room downstairs. It was barely 7:00 a.m., but he shouldn't have been surprised that his sister had heard he was back and was ready for a fight. He sighed and threw on a collared shirt and dress pants.

"Maya," he greeted his sister as he walked into the dining room. His parents' penthouse suite spanned the better part of the top floor of the forty-story building, plus a portion of the two floors below. The dining room was on the topmost floor and had a floor-to-ceiling view of Central Park. The staff had set out coffee and pastries. His parents were late risers and typically didn't come down to breakfast until 8:00 a.m.

His sister was five-seven and dressed like the New York power broker she was in a smart white dress suit that looked like it should be on the cover of *Businessweek*. She gave him a warm hug and a kiss on the cheek. More so than his brother, Dev felt close to Maya; even when they were kids, he'd been both her best friend and protector. He'd vehemently disagreed with her choice of husband but had ultimately supported her because she'd asked him to. In fact, he couldn't think of a time when he hadn't done what she'd asked.

"I see Dad couldn't live without you."

She poured him a cup of coffee with the amount of cream he liked and selected his favorite chocolate croissant from the pastry basket that his parents' staff had set out for them.

He sighed. "Apparently your husband can't live without you."

She looked down, tears shining in her eyes. "That's why I came early. I wanted to talk to you before Ma and Dad wake up. I need your help, Dev. I don't want to put you in an awkward position, I know you're supposed to have this time to explore your dreams, but I really need my big brother right now."

His stomach turned. Maya was tough as nails. Whatever was going on was bad, and his sister needed him.

His phone rang. He looked down at the display. It was Caitlyn. He looked at Maya's teary face. He couldn't take the call. He silenced it.

"Hey, Maya, you know I'm here for you. Whatever you need."

Twenty

He wasn't answering her call. She hung up without leaving a message. A deep ache settled into her chest. Everything she'd been trying to ignore came rising to the surface and soured her mouth.

Yes, he'd called her last night, but to say what? That all it had taken was for his father to show up and he'd left without even saying goodbye?

She walked to the windows to stare out at the neighboring ranch. She watched the cattle grazing in the fields. What was Dev doing? Was he looking out at the Manhattan skyline wondering how foolish he'd been to think he could live in Texas?

Tears streamed down her face. Her phone rang and she looked down eagerly, only to find it was Alice. She answered, hoping Alice had some information about why Dev had left so suddenly, a small part of her hoping there was a family emergency that had compelled him.

Alice insisted Caitlyn come over to her house. When Caitlyn appeared at her door, Alice pulled her inside and gave her a long hug.

"Darlin', I'm so sorry."

Caitlyn hadn't realized just how much she'd been holding in, because suddenly her body was racked with sobs. Alice held on to her. When her tears finally subsided, Alice put her on the comfortable couch and went to make them coffee. Caitlyn remembered that the last time she'd been sitting on that couch, Dev had walked through the door. It was the first time she'd seen him, and she'd nearly spit out her wine. Was it just three weeks ago that her biggest problem was that she had trouble talking to men and needed boyfriend lessons?

Alice returned with a steaming cup of coffee and handed it to Caitlyn, then sat beside her. Caitlyn curled her legs underneath her and turned to face Alice.

"Dev called Russ last night when he couldn't get hold of you. He had to go back to New York with his dad."

Caitlyn nodded and took a sip of the coffee to see if she could loosen the lump in her throat.

"Russ said he was really broken up about it and was even debating showing up at your house, but Russ talked him out of it. He didn't want him getting shot prowling around your house in the middle of the night."

"What was so urgent?" Caitlyn managed to choke out.

Alice shrugged. "He didn't say, just that he had to leave but he would call you."

"You were right all along." She filled Alice in on the conversation she'd had with Dev's mother and the disastrous meeting with his father the day before.

"I think your boyfriend's father mistakin' you for a hooker beats me sleeping with a guy who took a call from his mama while we were having sex," Alice joked, and it brought a small smile to Caitlyn's face.

"I didn't even know you owned a dress like that."

Caitlyn smiled wistfully. "I didn't. I bought it just for him. I refused to even go out to dinner looking like that."

Alice rubbed her arm. "For what it's worth, Russ said he's never seen Dev like this with any other woman. I think his feelings are genuine."

"It doesn't change the fact that his responsibilities are to his family."

"And what about yours?" Alice asked gently.

"What do you mean?"

"If Dev had gotten hold of you last night and asked you to come with him to New York to sort out his family drama, would you have gone?"

The question slammed into Caitlyn like a freight train at full speed. She didn't even have to think about it. She filled Alice in on the meeting they'd had with the private investigator. "We can't keep hoping that claim isn't legal. I have to be there for my family. This is devastating them. Even Alexa flew in this morning."

They were silent for a while, then Alice finally spoke. "I'm your friend, and one hundred percent on your side. But don't you think it's hypocritical to expect Dev to drop his family obligations when you're not willing to do the same? He's the eldest son, and you're the baby of the family. Imagine the pressure he's feeling."

Alice had just voiced what Caitlyn had always known deep down inside. She was asking Dev to make a sacrifice that she herself wasn't willing to make.

Her phone buzzed, and she looked down to see that Dev had texted. Tried to reach you. Had to come back to New York. I'll call you soon. I promise.

Alice leaned over to read the text. "You need to talk to him."

Caitlyn shook her head. She wiped the tears that had fallen on her phone and typed, I can't talk about this. I understand why you had to leave. I love you and always will, but we were foolish to think we could make this work between us. Your life is in New York and mine in Royal.

Alice placed a hand on Caitlyn's. "You can't send that text. You have to talk to him."

Caitlyn shook her head. "What good will that do? I thought talking to Jax would help me come to terms with our relationship, but the only thing it did is sow more doubt about my bad relationship skills." She wiped the tears from her face. "What will Dev say? That he loves me but that his family comes first? And what will I say back to him? That my family is more important than his? That he needs to give up his family obligations when I'm not willing to do the same?"

Alice took both their coffee cups and set them on the table. She hugged Caitlyn, who cried into her friend's shoulder.

The only thing left to do was to was accept the fact that the love of her life was gone.

Dev looked at the text Caitlyn had sent and cursed under his breath.

"Did you see the biodata of Anjali Verma?" his mother asked from across the breakfast table. His father was sitting at the head of the table, his face hidden behind the *New York Times*. As far as Vishvanath Mallik was concerned, the matter of Caitlyn had closed when he'd gotten Dev to agree to come back to New York.

Dev set his fork down on the plate with unnecessary force, and it clanked loudly enough to get his father's attention. Maya had already left, and while Dev had agreed to help her, he couldn't deal with her problem until he addressed his own.

"Ma, you can send the biodata for every girl around the globe, I'm not going to look at them and I'm not going to marry any of them."

His father sighed. "Is it about that girl?"

"Caitlyn is the love of my life," Dev said, not bothering to hide his anger.

"Dev, you know that we are very modern-thinking parents, but the one request we have is that you marry someone Indian," his mother said quietly.

Dev took a breath. "Ma, you've always taught me that the most important part of our culture is our family values. That we take care of each other, and are always there for each other."

"And an American girl can't understand that. How many of your *gori* girlfriends understood why you were still living at home? How many of them would be comfortable with us living with you in our old age?"

"That's what I'm trying to tell you, Ma. Do you know that Caitlyn lives at home with her parents? That she works day and night to make her family's business successful?"

"It's not the same. Indian girls have a different level of respect for their elders that I've never known American girls to have."

"Actually, Ma, you're mistaken if you think that just because a woman is Indian, she's okay with the concept of a joint family. The last girl you set me up with—remember Priya, who I went out with for a few weeks?"

His mother nodded enthusiastically. Priya was one of the few women that Dev had agreed to meet from the endless biodatas his mother sent. She was an NYU law student, and Dev had thought she sounded interesting.

"I liked Priya. Her mother just called me last

month to say that she's still single," his mother said encouragingly.

"Well, I'm not surprised. She specifically told me that she had no interest in being with a man whose life revolves around his family and that she will never agree to live with my or her own parents. She thinks her grandparents ruined her childhood. Oh, and she also doesn't want any children, and she'd like a husband who is willing to fly around the world with her, because she's going into international law and expects to have clients all over the globe."

Even as he said the words out loud, a thought he'd buried deep in the recesses of his brain surfaced. Wasn't he hoping Caitlyn would do the same thing? Wasn't he planning to open a national chain of restaurants and go from city to city setting up his business?

His mother gasped. "*Hai*, what a liar Priya's mother is. She assured me that she raised her daughter with very strong family values. Don't worry, the biodata I sent today, that girl…"

"You're not hearing me, Ma!"

His mother gaped at him. His father cleared his throat then slapped a hand down on the table, making the cutlery rattle on the plates. "We are not going to argue endlessly." His voice dropped. "Let me put it this way, Dev. You have a choice to make. That girl or us. You decide who is more important to you."

Dev sank back into his chair. He hadn't thought his parents would go this far, but they had, and with it, they'd sealed his fate.

Twenty-One

Caitlyn sighed when she saw who was calling. For the last week since Dev had left, she'd spent most of the time either wallowing in self-pity or tediously going through her grandfather's papers, a task no one else seemed to want to do. It suited her just fine, she didn't want to be around people. She'd canceled several meetings and even postponed her volunteer shift at the children's services center. She didn't need another reminder of how spectacularly she'd failed. The only thing she'd accomplished this week was to help Alexa with sorting out the family papers in preparation for the battle that was coming with the Thurstons' claim.

She answered her phone. "Hi, Greg."

"Miss Caitlyn, I'm glad I got hold of you."

Caitlyn didn't even have the energy to correct him.

"You remember those two horses at the Frederick ranch you called me about?"

Caitlyn sat up. "Yes. Did you talk to the ranch hand about brushing them more often, and making sure that—"

Greg cut her off. "Yes…the new owner asked if you would possibly meet him at the ranch today round 7:00 p.m. to tell him what he needs to do with the horses. He's never owned horses before."

Caitlyn sighed. It was probably one of the city people from Houston or Dallas who showed up in Royal thinking they'd like a country house. She had seen too many of them who liked the idea of owning horses and then trusted ranch hands to take care of them. She'd rescued four horses who had been neglected like the ones at the Fredrick ranch.

She was inclined to say no but then thought of the horses. She didn't want them suffering because she was too busy mourning Dev to help them.

"I'll be there."

"Thank you, Miss Caitlyn."

She hung up and got herself out of bed just as someone knocked on her door. She opened it to find Alexa. Her sister was dressed in black pants and a light blue top—her lawyer clothes.

"Wake up, sleepyhead." She smiled. "I came to say goodbye. I'm going home."

"Aren't you already home?" Caitlyn said, rubbing her eyes.

"Cute. Anyhow, one of my clients has an emergency, and I need to go back."

"But what about the Thurston claim?"

"I don't have to be here physically to work on it. I'll come back when needed." She put her hands on Caitlyn's shoulders. "You know my life is in Miami, right? I've already been here too long. I need to go back."

Caitlyn nodded. She'd hoped her sister would come back for good, but she'd made her own life in Miami. Alexa had never let anything stand in the way of getting what she wanted.

"I'll be here to help with whatever you need." She hated how sad her voice sounded.

"Hey, Caitlyn." Alexa sat on the bed beside her and placed an arm around her. "Please don't stay here if you're not happy." She sighed. "I've always worried that we dump too much on you. Don't for one second give up your dreams because you're feeling stuck here." She pulled back and met Caitlyn's gaze. "Go out and do what you want. Open your horse camp. Go to New York and be with Dev. It's not all on you. Jonathan and Jayden are here."

After Alexa left, Caitlyn thought about her words as she showered. In the last week, she'd missed all her board meetings, and the world still went on. She'd managed to take care of things over email. Maybe the new ranch owner wanting to meet her was a blessing in disguise. Perhaps she could offer to buy the ranch from him, or rent the stables to open her horse camp. Then another idea struck her. She dressed for the day and got to work. She'd been working on the wrong goal this whole time.

She didn't need a boyfriend, and she was done mourning Dev. It was time for her to focus on what was really important.

She arrived at the ranch a few minutes early. A rental car was parked in the driveway. Her heart contracted painfully as she drove up to the house. She'd loved it since the moment she'd seen it. It would make someone a nice home. She couldn't bring herself to go inside. Since she was an invited guest, she decided to take a chance on it being okay for her to walk to the back. She strolled toward the horses. They were turned out in the ring. She spoke softly as she approached, and the appaloosa seemed to remember her. He came trotting over. She snatched some clover from the ground and held it out. He ate from her hand. The mustang came over, eager for his share.

"You two are looking a little better. I'm glad the new owner talked to your ranch hand." The troughs inside the ring were full of clean water. It was crazy that this was only her second meeting with these horses. She didn't even know their names, and yet she knew this wouldn't be her last visit with them.

"Their names are Smoke and Shadow."

She whirled. There was no way he was here.

Twenty-Two

Dev loved the look on her face when she turned around. The sun was still high in the sky, and it shone down on her like spun gold. Her hair was pulled back in a ponytail. She wore a V-neck T-shirt and jeans, and even though it had only been a week, it felt like he'd been away from her for a lifetime.

He hadn't responded to her last text, knowing that he owed her more than a text or a phone call. No matter how things turned out between them, he wasn't going to be a jerk like her ex. He was not going to let this all end without letting her know just how amazing she was and helping her make her horse camp come true.

She stared at him as he approached. Her face was

inscrutable, and his stomach clenched. She couldn't even spare a smile for him?

"What are you doing here? Why have you returned now?" She looked away from him but he kept walking towards her. When he was standing before her, she looked him in the eyes.

"Did you think I wouldn't be back? Do you think so little of me?" He moved closer but she took a step back.

"Let's not make this harder than it already is. You and I both know that it was never going to work between us. Your father's visit just hastened what would've happened anyway."

"Please let me explain why I had to go. I was never leaving for good."

"Not then, but eventually you will." She looked away from him and he wanted to reach out and touch her but wasn't sure how she'd react.

He rubbed the back of his neck. This conversation wasn't going the way he had planned at all. He hated the way she was looking at him, her eyes full of pain and mistrust.

"I bought this place for you," he blurted out.

Her head snapped up "What do you mean?"

"The night before I left. I bought this place. It's in your name. I bought it for you. No business partnership, no strings attached—it's for your horse camp. Or for you to do with as you want."

She stepped back another pace, her back now against the horse ring. Smoke, the appaloosa, trotted over and nuzzled against her neck. Her eyes were locked on Dev's. She didn't even notice the horse.

"So what is this? A goodbye present?"

Her tone was a punch to his gut. Was that what she thought he was doing? "No. I thought... It's..." He took a breath. "I bought this place for you so you'd know that you are under no obligation..."

"Why would I be obliged to you?"

Everything was coming out all wrong. He should just do what he came to do.

Stepping back, he dropped his knees.

Her eyes widened.

"Caitlyn, you are the love of my life. From the moment I saw you, I knew there was a connection between us. I've loved you from that first night at Alice's house, and since then my love has only grown and solidified. You are kind, you are caring, you are intelligent and being with you has given me the kind of strength I've never had on my own. I don't want to live without you."

He realized he didn't have the ring in his hand, and he pulled it out of his pocket. "This ring belonged to my *nani*, my maternal grandmother. She gave it to my mother to give to my future wife. I came here to ask if you'd marry me."

Caitlyn was staring at him, her eyes shining. Had she decided that she didn't want to be with him?

"How do we make it work between us? How do we split our lives? The first time your father showed up, you dropped everything and left." His heart stopped. Her voice seemed to be coming from far away even though she was only a foot away from him. Had he messed this all up? Had he taken too long to sort things out with his family?

"I'm sorry, Caitlyn. I didn't know how best to handle things. I needed to go, to put things to rest with my family so I could come back here to you. You have to forgive me."

"Where are we going to live? How are we going to make this work, Dev? Love doesn't conquer all. We can't keep ignoring these things."

He was still on his knees. Picturing this moment was what had kept him going through the last week. It was what had given him the strength to stand up to his family. But what he'd dreamed of was her screaming yes and flying into his arms. Had he miscalculated so badly? His knees were wet from the soft ground, and his joints were stiff as he stood. He didn't put the ring away.

He took a step toward her. She placed her hands behind her on the fence, and he retreated.

"I was hoping you might let me live here with you. I'm thinking this would make a really great house for us, and these barns would be great for your camp. I'll open my restaurant at that old Stevens brewery. I'll make it work. If you let me, Caitlyn, we will live right here in Royal, where you can be close to your family."

She shook her head. "I can't do that to you. I won't. I won't take you away from your family. It'll be fine at first, but then you'll resent me. You'll hate the fact that I stuck you in this town, that I took you away from your dreams."

It was time to give up hope that he was going to get his picture-perfect proposal. What he hadn't really thought about was what he would do if she said no. He put the ring back in his pocket.

"I've thought this through. This town will be my flagship restaurant. Then I'll open the chain I was planning. I'll have to travel a lot, and that's something you'll have to put up with. I promise when I come back, I'll make it up to you." He gave her a smile, and his heart skipped a little when she smiled back and took one small step toward him.

"It's not fair for you to give up everything. Your dreams, your family. Why do you want to do that?"

"My dreams have changed Caitlyn, there is nothing I want more than you. If this last week has taught me anything, it's that I can't live without you."

She took another step toward him and held out her arms, palms down. He took her hands, desperate with the need to touch her. Her eyes shone.

"I can't let you do that."

"I want to."

She shook her head. "That's not how it works in a relationship. My family can figure things out without me. My sister, Alexa, lives in Miami. She's here when the family needs her, but she has her own life. I can do the same."

"What about your horse camp?"

"That I'm not willing to give up. But I also don't

have to do everything by myself for it. I can steal a ranch hand or two from my father and delegate. The important thing is to have a place for the kids to go, I don't personally have to teach them to ride every day."

What is she saying? "You want to give up your family and your camp for me?"

She smiled. "It's not a matter of sacrificing or giving things up—it's making things work. If you reduce some of your family responsibilities, and I reprioritize my time, we can make this work. In fact, I just resigned from several of my board seats today. There are any number of people who can fill those seats, but there is only one person who can make me happy."

His heart was pounding so wildly in his chest, he was sure it was about to burst. He pulled her close and she came willingly, lifting her chin so he could bend down and kiss her. He kissed her softly, savoring the feel of her lips. "I love you, Caitlyn. I'll do whatever it takes to make it work."

"I still haven't forgiven you for leaving me."

His heart lurched. "Tell me how I can make it up to you. Tell me what I need to do for you to forgive me."

She smiled and stepped back from him. "There is no forgiving you for what you put me through this last week. You're going to have to spend your whole life making it up to me."

Wait, what?

"Does this mean you'll—" He didn't get to finish his thought, because she stood on her tiptoes and pulled his head down, pressing her lips to his.

Twenty-Three

"I'm the only guy here not wearing a cowboy hat," Dev said. "You could've lent me one."

Caitlyn laughed. "Don't worry, I'm sure we'll find some here."

"So what is this place, exactly?"

"It's the Texas Cattleman's Club. Each year they throw this summer barbecue. Everyone who is anyone in Royal will be here, and you're going to have to meet them if you want that restaurant of yours to be a success."

The barbecue was set up on the sprawling lawns of the Texas Cattleman's Club. The day was hot, but a cool front had come in the night before, so there was a slight breeze. A giant white tent held cooling fans, but most everyone seemed to prefer it outside. The air smelled of smoked meat and whiskey.

"Caitlyn, tell me what I'm seeing on your finger is not an engagement ring!" Caitlyn turned to see Chelsea Grandin.

She smiled. "Meet my fiancé, Dev Mallik."

Chelsea smiled at him. "It's nice to see you again. Now let me see that ring." She tugged on Caitlyn's hand and inspected the ring. Chelsea was wearing a summer dress with cowboy boots, her long hair loose around her shoulders. "It's a really unusual stone. Is that a pink diamond?"

"Dev, you have to tell the story. When I first heard it, I started crying." It *was* an unusual ring, with a round-cut stone that had pink and orange hues depending on how the light hit it. The huge stone was set in a simple yellow gold band which just made it look even bigger. Her mother had fanned herself when she saw it, claiming it had to be around ten carats. She'd grilled Dev, who had no idea how many carats the ring was, and then proceeded to tell the story of how he'd gotten the ring.

"The stone is a padparadscha sapphire. They are rare sapphires that are mined in Sri Lanka. My *nani*—that's my mother's mother—was born in Sri Lanka. Her family emigrated to India to flee the famine in Sri Lanka. They had very few possessions, but the one thing they did have was this stone, which was originally set in a necklace that had been gifted to my great-grandfather by the mine owner in return for saving his life from a rockslide. My *nani* was the eldest child, and she wore it around her neck for safekeeping. She had two brothers and a sister, but they all died either during the travel or immediately afterward from disease. My *nani* is the only one who survived. She always held the belief that the stone protected her. Anyhow, she died last year, but before she did, she gave the necklace to my mother and asked her to reset it into a ring and save it for my future wife. Since she knew she wouldn't see me married, she wanted to give this stone as a way of giving our marriage her blessing."

Chelsea put a hand to her heart. "I will not lie, I am so jealous of you right now." They chatted for a few more minutes, then she gave Caitlyn a hug and left to socialize.

Dev steered her toward the tent. It was mostly empty, and the bar inside had no line. They each got a glass of wine. The last few days had been a blissful blur. After she'd accepted his marriage proposal, they'd gone back to her house to announce it to her family. Alexa had offered to fly home, but Caitlyn told her to stay put. She'd have to come home soon enough for whatever happened next with the Thurston claim. Caitlyn hadn't wanted her sister to run herself ragged flying back and forth.

She and Dev had picked out furniture for the Fredrick ranch, which they'd promptly decided to rename Smoke and Shadow, after the horses. Ol'Fred had helped Dev get a contractor, who was going to remodel the old Stevens brewery for his restaurant.

They found a quiet corner. "We've been so busy,

you haven't told me how you convinced your dad to make Maya the CEO of his business."

Dev smiled. "A combination of pleading, begging, threatening and cajoling." He took a sip of his wine. "Remember I told you that when I came to Royal, my sister had taken over dealing with the business. Well, the reason my dad came to get me is that Maya's husband had called him saying that his and Maya's marriage was on the verge of divorce because she was spending so much time in the office."

"But you were only gone for three weeks. That can't have been the sole reason."

He nodded. "It wasn't. Maya came to me the morning I arrived. Her marriage has been on the rocks for a while. She gave up everything she wanted to do with her career to help her husband deal with his family responsibilities. She hasn't been happy with her life for a while now, and getting back to work just reminded her of what she really wants out of life. She wants a divorce, and she needed my help to get it."

"Why did she need you?"

"Because she will be the first person in my family to ever get a divorce. It's not done in Indian families—at least not traditional ones like ours. Maya doesn't want to be estranged from my parents. I had to support her and convince them that Maya's happiness is what's most important to us."

"I'm so sorry. I wish you'd told me before you left. I would've understood."

"I know you would. But at that time, there was so

much to deal with in my family, I wasn't thinking straight. It took Maya and me some time to make my parents see that their stubbornness would've caused Maya lifelong grief. But in a way, getting them to see why Maya was unhappy helped my case."

Caitlyn smirked. "Did your mother mistake Maya's husband for a male escort?"

He laughed. "No, that honor will forever remain yours." She punched him playfully. "In all seriousness, they realized that their insistence on Maya marrying someone Indian had led her to choose the wrong the person. I told Maya about you, and she convinced my mother that she could be happy for us and have the opportunity to interfere in our lives, or hold on to her stubbornness and lose me. On the day I was scheduled to leave, she showed up with the ring and asked me to give it to you."

"Dad was really impressed that you asked him first."

Dev smiled. "That's how it's done in Indian culture. My mother would have never forgiven me. It was a bit of a challenge to come see your dad without you finding out."

"Wait, you came to my house?"

He nodded. "Around the time Alexa was leaving. She was dispatched to your room to keep you busy while I snuck in the house to go meet your dad."

"I can't believe Alexa didn't tell me. And she knew how miserable I was without you."

"Yeah, your dad did make me promise that I would make sure he never had to see that mopey look on your face. He also made me promise that I would propose that day, which was a bummer because I had this whole plan that I couldn't put into action."

"And what was that?"

He grinned. "Well, in Indian weddings, the groom rides in on a horse. So, I was going to get the ranch hand to saddle up Smoke for me, and I was going to ride him."

"Do you know how to ride a horse?"

He shook his head. "No, but I wasn't going for a race around the town. I figured I could just sit on him and have him walk a few steps."

Caitlyn sighed. "There is so much I'm going to have to teach you. Starting with the fact that you can't just get on a horse and ride him."

Dev leaned over and pressed his lips to hers. "I look forward to you teaching me all kinds of things." She couldn't resist kissing him back. Since he'd returned, she couldn't get enough of him.

"I see you two have kissed and made up."

Caitlyn turned to see Heath Thurston, and she tensed. Alexa had specifically told them not to speak to him.

Dev held out his hand. "Hey, man, I'm sorry about that night. I was out of line."

Heath took Dev's hand and shook it. "It's okay. I could tell just by looking at the two of you that there was something hot and heavy going on, and I wasn't going to get in the middle of that."

Caitlyn politely excused them and dragged Dev

outside. "What is going on with you and that guy?" Dev said.

"That's Heath Thurston, the guy who's making the claim against the ranch."

Dev raised his brows. "Well, then, it's a good thing I rescued you from him the other night."

Caitlyn rolled her eyes.

"Wait, if that guy was Heath, who's that guy talking to your friend?" Dev gestured toward a grassy knoll. The tent door where Heath had gone in was behind them.

Caitlyn turned to look where Dev had pointed, and the sip of wine she'd just taken came spurting out of her mouth. "Oh my God!"

She'd dribbled some on her dress. Dev dabbed at her dress with a napkin. "I guess we're going to have to take you home and get that dress off," he said with a sparkle in his eyes.

Normally she'd be embarrassed, but she was too distracted with what she was seeing. Chelsea Grandin seemed to be in a heavy conversation with a guy who looked exactly like Heath. But Heath was in the tent.

"That's Nolan Thurston, Heath's twin brother."

Caitlyn tried not to stare, but it was impossible. Chelsea was standing close to Nolan, and he was whispering in her ear.

"Those two look awfully chummy. Especially after Alexa told you guys not to talk to the Thurstons."

Caitlyn nodded. What was Chelsea up to? She

remembered her own encounter with Heath at the bar. She'd thought she could flirt with him and get information. Was Chelsea doing the same? Didn't she understand how dangerous the game was? After all, Dev was only supposed to have been giving her boyfriend lessons, and here she was engaged to him.

Then another thought struck her. "The Grandins have a lot more to lose than we do. If Ashley is Daniel's daughter, the Thurstons have a blood tie to the Grandins."

"Listen, I've seen this happen in a lot of families. I know your family is friends with the Grandins, but you need to watch out. When it comes to the family home, people will do anything to protect what's theirs."

She nodded. She would call Alexa. They needed to know what Chelsea and Nolan were up to.

"Now, it's nice to see that smile on your face." Ol'Fred interrupted her thoughts, and she grinned at him. "I assume this fella is the reason?" She nodded and held out her hand for Ol'Fred to inspect. "Well, that's a nice sapphire. A rare one, too."

Caitlyn laughed. "Trust you to know jewelry, too."

"So when's the big day? I hav'ta plan for all the fancy stuff you're gonna need."

Caitlyn looked at Dev, who looked back at her. The sooner the better, as far as she was concerned. They had both decided that they weren't going to wait for the wedding to begin their lives. She was flying to New York next week to meet with his parents—the right way. The permits for her horse camp had been filed. Smoke and Shadow were going to make great riding horses, and she'd put out the word in the community for old horses that would make for good trail riders.

"It'll be soon," Dev said. "I can't wait to make Caitlyn my wife."

After Ol'Fred had left, Caitlyn kissed him. "How about we leave this shindig and go practice being husband and wife?"

* * * * *

Don't miss the next book in the
Texas Cattleman's Club: Ranchers and Rivals

On Opposite Sides
by Cat Schield

HARLEQUIN

DESIRE

#2881 ON OPPOSITE SIDES
Texas Cattleman's Club: Ranchers and Rivals
by Cat Schield
Determined to save her family ranch, Chelsea Grandin launches a daring scheme to seduce Nolan Thurston to discover his family's plans—and he does the same. Although they suspect they're using one another, their schemes disintegrate as attraction takes over...

#2882 ONE COLORADO NIGHT
Return to Catamount • by Joanne Rock
Cutting ties with her family, developer Jessamyn Barclay returns to the ranch to make peace, not expecting to see her ex, Ryder Wakefield. When one hot night changes everything, will they reconnect for their baby's sake or will a secret from the past ruin everything?

#2883 AFTER HOURS TEMPTATION
404 Sound • by Kianna Alexander
Focused on finishing an upcoming album, sound engineer Teagan Woodson and guitarist Maxton McCoy struggle to keep things professional as their attraction grows. But agreeing to "just a fling" may lead to *everything* around them falling apart...

#2884 WHEN THE LIGHTS GO OUT...
Angel's Share • by Jules Bennett
A blackout at her distillery leaves straitlaced Elise Hawthorne in the dark with her potential new client, restaurateur Antonio Rodriguez. One kiss leads to more, but everything is on the line when the lights come back on...

#2885 AN OFFER FROM MR. WRONG
Cress Brothers • by Niobia Bryant
Desperately needing a buffer between him and his newly discovered family, chef and reluctant heir Lincoln Cress turns to the one person who's all wrong for him—the PI who uncovered this information, Bobbie Barnett. But this fake relationship reveals very real desire...

#2886 HOW TO FAKE A WEDDING DATE
Little Black Book of Secrets • by Karen Booth
Infamous for canceling her million-dollar nuptials, Alexandra Gold is having a *little* trouble finding a date to the wedding of the season. Enter her brother's best friend, architect Ryder Carson. He's off-limits, so he's *safe*—except for the undeniable sparks between them!

HDCNM0522

SPECIAL EXCERPT FROM

HQN

*Welcome to Four Corners Ranch, Maisey Yates's
newest miniseries, where the West is still wild...and
when a cowboy needs a wife, he decides to find her
the old-fashioned way!*

*Evelyn Moore can't believe she's agreed to uproot her city
life to become Oregon cowboy and single dad
Sawyer Garrett's mail-order bride. Her love for his tiny
daughter is instant. Her feelings for Sawyer are...more
complicated. Her gruff cowboy husband ignites a thrilling
desire in her, but Sawyer is determined to keep their
marriage all about the baby. But what happens if
Evelyn wants it all?*

The front door opened, and a man came out. He had on a black cowboy hat, and he was holding a baby. Those were the first two details she took in, but then there was… Well, there was the whole rest of him.

Evelyn could feel his eyes on her from some fifty feet away, could see the piercing blue color. His nose was straight and strong, as was his jaw. His lips were remarkable, and she didn't think she had ever really found lips on a man all that remarkable. He had the sort of symmetrical good looks that might make a man almost too pretty, but he was saved from that by a scar that edged through the corner of his mouth, creating a thick white line that disrupted the symmetry there. He was tall. Well over six feet, and broad.

And his arms were…

Good Lord.

He was wearing a short-sleeved black T-shirt, and he cradled the tiny baby in the crook of a massive bicep and forearm. He could easily lift bales of hay and throw them around. Hell, he could probably easily lift the truck and throw it around.

He was beautiful. Objectively, absolutely beautiful.

But there was something more than that. Because as he walked toward her, she felt like he was stealing increments of her breath, emptying her lungs. She'd seen handsome men before. She'd been around celebrities who were touted as the sexiest men on the planet.

But she had never felt anything quite like this.

Because this wasn't just about how he looked on the outside, though it was sheer masculine perfection; it was about what he did to her insides. Like he had taken the blood in her veins and replaced it with fire. And she could say with absolute honesty she had never once in all of her days wanted to grab a stranger and fling herself at him, and push them both into the nearest closet, bedroom, whatever, and…

Well, everything.

But she felt it, right then and there with him.

And there was something about the banked heat in his blue eyes that made her think he might feel exactly the same way.

And suddenly she was terrified of all the freedom. Giddy with it, which went right along with that joy/terror paradox from before.

She didn't know anyone here. She had come without anyone's permission or approval. She was just here. With this man. And there was nothing to stop them from…anything.

Except he was holding a baby and his sister was standing right to her left. But otherwise…

She really hoped that he was Sawyer. Because if he was Wolf, it was going to be awkward.

"Evelyn," he said. And goose bumps broke out over her arms. And she knew. Because he was the same man who had told her that she would be making him meat loaf whether she liked it or not.

And suddenly the reason it had felt distinctly sexual this time became clear.

"Yes," she responded.

"Sawyer," he said. "Sawyer Garrett." And then he absurdly took a step forward and held his hand out. To shake. And she was going to have to… touch him. Touch him and not melt into a puddle at his feet.

Find out what happens next in Evelyn and Sawyer's marriage deal in Unbridled Cowboy, *the unmissable first installment in Maisey Yates's new Four Corners Ranch miniseries.*

Don't miss Unbridled Cowboy *by New York Times bestselling author Maisey Yates, available May 2022 wherever HQN books and ebooks are sold.*

HQNBooks.com